A LOVE THAT CROSSES TIME

Maria's Book

Also By Holly Fourchalk

Adrenal Fatigue: Why am I so tired all the time?

Are you what you eat? Why Your Intestines Are The Foundation of Good Health

Cancer: Why what you don't know about your treatment could harm you.

Depression: The Real Cause May Be Your Body.

Diabetes: What Your Physician Doesn't Know

Glutathione: Your Body's Secret Healing Agent

Your Heart: Are you taking care of it?

Inflammation: The Silent Killer

Managing Your Weight: Why your body may be working against you and what you can do about it

The Chocolate Controversy: The Bad, the Mediocre and the Awesome

So What's the Point: If You Have Ever Asked

Your Immune System: Is Yours Protecting You?

Your Vital Liver: How to protect your liver from life's toxins

The Entwined Collection
Entwined: A Romantic Journey Back into Health

Entwined: The Ongoing Journey

Tom's Collection
The Cosmic Socialite

All of the above are available at
www.DrHollyBooks.com

A LOVE THAT CROSSES TIME
Maria's Book

Holly Fourchalk
PhD., DNM®, RHT, AAP

Cover design by Peter Forde. Editing by Christine Pollock. Publishing by Leah Albrecht.

Choices Unlimited for Health & Wellness
Dr. Holly Fourchalk, Ph.D., DNM®, RHT, HT
Tel: 604.764.5203
Websites: www.ChoicesUnlimited.ca
         www.DrHollyBooks.com
E-mail: holly@choicesunlimited.ca

ISBN 978-1-7752425-8-1 (softcover)
ISBN 978-1-7752425-9-8 (ebook)

Disclaimer

This book is an attempt to increase awareness about health and the many options we have to bring the body back into a healthy balance.

Every effort has been made, by the author, to ensure the information in this book is as accurate as possible. However, it is by no means a complete, or exhaustive, examination of all information.

The author believes in prevention and the superiority of a natural non-invasive approach to health over synthetic drugs and/or surgery.

As a Doctor of Natural Medicine, a researcher and teacher, the author knows what has worked for others and what worked for her. However, because our bodies are unique, any two individuals may experience different results from the same therapy. No two people are the same and the author cannot, and does not, render judgment or advice regarding a particular individual's situation.

The information collected within comes from a variety of researchers and sources from around the world. This information has been accumulated in the Western healing arts over the past thirty years.

Research shows the top three leading causes of death in North America occurs directly from the physician/ pharmaceutical component. However, could the real leading underlying cause of death and disability be attributed to the lack of awareness of the natural REAL therapies?

These therapies are proven and well known to prevent and treat many common degenerative, inflammatory and oxidative diseases.

Today ever-increasing numbers of people are aware of healing foods and herbs, supplements and modalities, but there are still far too many who are not. The fact that our physicians are part of this latter group makes healing even more challenging. Adding to this, another unfortunate fact is those who can profit from sickness and disease promote ignorance, creating devastating results.

Today we are seeing more and more laboratories and universities around the world, studying herbs, nutrition and various healing modalities with phenomenal success.

It is not the intent of the author that anyone should choose to read this book; make self-diagnosed decisions regarding their health; and treat themselves. But rather, that people recognize the various options that are available and find a good health practitioner to work with.

It is the responsibility of the individual to find good professional health care practitioners to work with to resolve health issues and achieve optimal health.

The author and publisher are not responsible for any adverse effects or consequences resulting from the use of any of the suggestions, or information, contained in the book but offer this material as information the public has a right to hear and utilize at its own discretion.

To my Parents

For all their support and encouragement
My Dad for his ever listening ear
My Mother for her open mind

Contents

Preface

Before we explore what, The Entwined Collection is about, let's begin by understanding where Dr. Holly is coming from; and how and why she wants everyone to benefit.

Dr. Holly was born with a genetic disorder. Her delivery was a confusion of issues that went wrong; some of which were not recognized at the time. Her petite mal, or absence, seizures started when she was 4 years old, though nobody recognized what was happening. Absence seizures are named for the brief loss of consciousness, and often misinterpreted as daydreaming.

At the age of nine, she was in a dramatic accident which provoked, and accelerated, her female development. It also provoked the myoclonic seizures which manifested themselves in powerful twitches or muscle jerks or spasms. By the time she was 14, the petite mal seizures and myoclonic seizures now included grand mal, or tonic-clonic, seizures.

The grand mal/tonic-clonic seizures, a type of generalized seizure, affected the entire brain. During these types of seizures, she would lose consciousness and the skeletal muscles would thrash violently and uncontrollably followed by amnesia, headaches, a damaged tongue and exhaustion.

After Holly's first grand mal seizure, her mother found her passed out on the floor and was devastated. She had already lost two children; she was not prepared to lose another. The problem became more complex. The more medication Holly was put on, the more seizures she had; never mind all the weight and other issues the medications caused. Four, five, six mornings out of seven she woke up with petite mal and myoclonic seizures. The medical profession blamed the car accident and increased both the number of drugs and their dosage, which of course provoked more seizures.

Struggling to resolve the seizures, her mother attended medical conferences, even though she didn't understand half of what they were saying. She booked Holly into Naturopaths, Reflexologists, and Acupuncturists, and anyone who thought they could stop the seizures. They even worked with Edgar Cayce remedies. They had to find a way to stop the seizures.

It wasn't until Holly was studying neurological issues in university that she recognized she had been having seizures since she was four years old.

Holly's favorite and most beloved practitioner was Dr. Loffler, an Osteopath/Naturopath, whom she started to see at the age of 18. He identified a number of issues compounding the problem going back to the car accident. Her second favorite physician was the neurologist she started see at the age of 26. She identified the genetic issue that was causing the seizures and other problems. Holly learned that people with this type of disorder didn't usually graduate from high school and were usually dead by the time they were 26 years old. In addition, her EEGs indicated she shouldn't be able to talk.

In university she was diagnosed with an ovarian tumor the size of a hard ball. She was told she needed surgery immediately as it was dangerous. Dr. Loffler, however, put her on a specific diet for ovarian tumors. Due to family pressure, she underwent a second laparotomy 3.5 weeks later. The tumor was gone. Her medical doctors never asked how she accomplished that.

At the age of 26, she burnt her eyes and the specialist told her she had to join classes to learn how to be blind as she would be legally blind by the time she was 30. She went back a year and half later with 20/19 vision. He never asked how she accomplished that.

In school, Dr. Holly had to deal with issues like ADD (Attention Deficit Disorder) and Dyslexia, yet she studied hard and diligently and always maintained her honor roll marks. She loved numbers and went into university hoping to get degrees in Physics and Math and become an Astrophysicist. However, that wasn't the plan life had for her and she came out as a Registered Psychologist. She ran her own practice for some 20 years.

During her training and practice as a psychologist, she was constantly frustrated at the total lack of training regarding the nutrients the brain required to function properly. Many of her clients came in with issues of depression and anxiety and other disorders. Dr. Holly would often suggest they see other practitioners like Naturopaths, Herbalists, or go for Hydro colonics. Repeatedly, supposed psychological issues were successfully solved, using other healing disciplines.

Dr. Holly attended Medical School as part of her of her first PhD, PsychoNeuroEndocrinology, which was in research and design. Two of the professors asked her to please stop asking questions. Why? Utilizing her knowledge in research and design; she repeatedly pointed out that referenced studies were not proving what they claimed. In fact, most of "evidenced based medicine" was not in fact, evidenced based – it was hypothesis based AND more and more of the hypotheses were being proven wrong. This was destroying the moral of the students.

Subsequently she learned how Big Pharma controls most Medical School Curriculums; and the Protocol and Procedure MDs are required to follow. In addition, they are now saying it can take up to 40 years for good research to get to the MDs and to the hospitals.

One thing Dr. Holly was never short on, was energy. Consequently, in addition to her academic profession and Psychology practice, Dr. Holly also opened and ran a big rig trucking company; an accounting business; a warehouse and distribution business and a rental company. However, she found herself challenged with the lack of morals and integrity in the trucking and warehousing businesses and eventually went back to school.

Dr. Holly got fed up with the limitations imposed on her within the field of psychology and enrolled in Naturopathic College. It was a double graduate program, 8 years completed in 4 years. Dr. Holly was also required to complete two years of Premed during the first year; meanwhile she continued her Psychology Practice.

By the time second year started, the seizures started up again. Very Scary. She hadn't had seizures for 15 years. In addition, other major health issues evolved. Her body kept telling her to quit. Holly was never a quitter. However, the College found out she was having seizures and put her on hold for a year. When she returned the following year, the seizures started up within three weeks, so she transferred from the Naturopathic program to a Doctor of Natural Medicine, wherein she could go at her own pace.

Holly went to India to complete, and intern for, for two Ayurveda medical programs. She also completed a Masters in Herbal Medicine: *Bridging Ayurveda, Traditional Chinese Medicine and Western Herbal Medicine*. She studied homeopathy and reflexology, locally and abroad. She then applied and was accepted for a PhD program in Nutrition where she received a Cum Laude for her thesis identifying the biochemistry of cellular healing.

During this time, Dr. Holly applied to, and was accepted, into Law School. She wanted to know the ins and outs of law to protect practitioners from their Colleges and from Big Pharma.

While completing the various degrees, Dr. Holly worked with a mentor as she prepared to leave the College of Psychologists. In the meantime, the College of Psychologists accused her of practicing "non-evidence based' medicine. She volunteered to provide workshops teaching the nutrients that the brain required to function from a nutritional and biochemistry perspective, but they were not interested. She left.

Her practice as a Dr. of Natural Medicine was up and running by this time. She published twelve books for the general public over the next four years. She wanted the general public to understand the differences between

Conventional Medicine/managing symptoms and REAL medicine/resolving the underlying issues.

The Entwined Collection

One day Dr. Holly woke up with an idea. Write a sexy romantic novel that would attract a larger audience, incorporating a huge amount of health information explaining REAL medicine and *Entwined: A Romantic Journey Back into Health* came to fruition.

Preparing to go away on a vacation and write the sequel to *Entwined*, Dr. Holly woke up with the idea of the Round Table and asking each character in the book to write their own book. This way, she could a use all the different literary genres to convey a huge amount of information on health and wellness. People could enjoy learning about REAL health and medicine reading the writing genre they preferred: educational, romantic, mystery, political, etc. Consequently, each book in the Entwined Book Collection is written with a different slant and from a different perspective according to the character of the Entwined Book Project responsible for the book.

 Dr. Holly attributes different healing disciplines to each of the Gibson family members who all work at the Gibson Clinic. With two exceptions: Dr. Holly is not a physiotherapist, and nor did she finish her Traditional Chinese Medicine program. Otherwise, Dr. Holly has all the degrees and designations to professionally address the issues focused on by her characters.

On a personal note, "**Entwined**" has a lot more meaning for Dr. Holly than just being the collection of books resulting from *Entwined: A Romantic Journey Back into Health*.

The word Entwined reflects life itself. All aspects of our beingness are entwined: from the moral/ethical; to the spiritual/religious; to the intellectual/emotional; to the physical/sexual; to the family/social; to the ingestion/elimination; and to all the different energetics. They are all **entwined**. In addition, the individual is entwined with their family; with their social network; with the community; and with the nation. Again, all is **entwined;** encompassing the local to the universal. Nothing happens in isolation; **entwined** embraces all, whether local or all matter stretching throughout the universe.

Consequently, when we look at our health and wellbeing, we need to take the whole being into consideration. To isolate any aspect of our being, whether it be our physical health, psychological health, energetic health, etc. is to negate an aspect of who we are.

Two powerful words for Dr. Holly are **Entwined** and **Choices**. Just as our health is immeasurably **entwined** with all of whom we are; so are all our **Choices Entwined** with what we choose to do with those choices. Whether it is our symptoms, our health, our relationships, our careers, etc., we can choose to manage, or we can choose to eliminate. The **CHOICE** is ours.

All of us involved in the writing, editing, publishing and marketing of these books, hope you enjoy the books; learn a lot from the books; and wish you the very best of health.

Maria's Book - A Love That Crosses Time

Join Maria as she brings together her loves of philosophical, religious and esoteric beliefs into a romantic novel. Three fascinating couples learn how to connect, in another dimension, across time. Each of whom is directed by a mentor, who helps them develop their gifts; opens doors of understanding and teaches a wealth of information.

In addition, the mentor teaches them how to go beyond time and space to learn and develop their careers.

Each book in the Entwined Collection is required to focus on health and wellness. So, Maria, creatively combines her love of herbal medicines utilized in different cultures, over time. Herbal medicine is the foundation of much of Western synthetic medicines and is still used in 80% of the world according to the WHO.

Chapter 1

Today

Today is a lovely day; perfect timing for a vacation in the Dominican Republic. It's late February, the rainy season has virtually passed. It usually lasted from mid-October to the end of January although from January through March, they could still have some good rainfalls, though typically just at night.

Days, like today, are perfect; the sun bathing, the water, and the beautiful sandy shores. It was a week day with hardly anyone on the beach; just the gentle lapping of the water against the sandy shoreline.

The rains this year were very good. The streets flooded, and the rivers overflowed. The vegetation was lush and green once again. If the Dominican Republic didn't get the rains the heavens provided each year, there would be a drought. The temperature remained about 30^0 C year-round. The population didn't enjoy or suffer, depending on how you looked at it, the seasons of the year, but they reveled in the much-appreciated rains.

Jasmine and Jordan lay on the beach. Both enjoyed their seasons at home, but they also enjoyed getting away to a hot climate to break up the winter. Actually, they enjoyed getting away any time of the year and loved going to different places whether for work or for pleasure.

They loved helping people and travelled around the world on volunteer projects. She was a physician and would help find ways to incorporate different cultures, their plants, their foods and their beliefs, to resolve their medical issues. He was a 'Green' architectural engineer and would find novel, creative ways of bringing much needed resources to the MASH style hospitals. After a few weeks or months of exhausting work, they would pamper themselves with a vacation through one of their time share programs. Their passion was exploring the different cultures, foods, agricultures and historical aspects of wherever they went. Then they would return home and work in their respective professions, until the next project came up.

Today it was beach time; nothing to do; nowhere to go; no one to see; just lay on the beach. The waters were a beautiful turquoise with the deeper blue waters out beyond. There was the odd fluffy cloud off in the distance with a gentle breeze coming off the ocean. It was perfect.

The last volunteer project they worked on in Haiti exhausted them physically and emotionally. In many of the places they had volunteered previously, and they volunteered around the world, the people were full of gratitude and appreciation. But many of the Haitian people had a lot of anger and resentment. They were a very hard-working people that had suffered from a series of very corrupt governments; consequently, most lived below the poverty line. The people's primary belief system was wrapped up in a very complex and deep complexity of

Catholicism and Voodoo. Both their beliefs and cultures were difficult to understand, and they were an exceedingly closed people. From a naïve Westerner's perspective, they seemed to have little respect for life, especially those in the more rural places. Their Voodoo practices often involved the human blood sacrifices. To get the human blood, they were known to chop off the hands, arms, legs, etc. they believed they needed for these sacrifices. You certainly didn't want to provoke anyone in any way and had to be very careful, watching everything you said and did, even the expressions on your face. And so, it became an emotionally exhausting project, working in an isolated rural area, in an entirely different way than they were accustomed to.

Here in the warmth of the sun and the safety of the Dominican, it was an entirely different world. The two cultures, side by side, evolved very differently.

In Haiti, the French and the Black slaves didn't really interact, and the two cultures had remained very separate. So, in many places, the Voodoo culture was alive and well, under the guise of Catholicism.

The history of the Dominican was different. In the Dominican, the Spanish and the Black slaves had interacted, and the Dominicans were now a very mixed race of people. The predominant belief system was Christianity without the Voodoo.

In the Dominican, the skin tones varied tremendously, from the various light tan browns to the deep darker browns; unlike Haiti, where it was 90% black, black, black.

Jasmin and Jordon lay on the beach, here in the north of the Dominican, in Puerto Plata. Puerto Plata is one of 32 provinces boasting beautiful, lazy beaches and during the week, there was hardly a soul in sight; a perfect beach to relax on. Jordan reached over and took Jasmine's hand in his, as they fell asleep under the warmth of the sun.

Chapter 2

A Long Time Before

Jordan and Jasmine met 20 years before at the same university. They were from different states; he from the East coast in Connecticut; and she from the West coast in Oregon. Both of their families had wanted them to go to the respective 'family' universities, but for some reason they had both been drawn to the University of Minnesota.

Jasmine went into medicine and Jordan went into architectural engineering. Both were very diligent committed students. Jordan loved working in the library. There was a senior professor who had taken a liking to him and often met with him in the library. He seemed to enjoy provoking Jordan with interesting and novel ideas. Jordan nicknamed him Professor Merlin because he seemed to have such a magical way of looking at things. Jordan often preferred to go to the library just to work with Professor Merlin rather than engage in the various socializations taking place amongst their peers.

Neither Jordan nor Jasmine wasted time and money on alcohol or experimented with drugs; neither had time for one-night stands or the young foolish or flirty kind of relationships their peers engaged in. Neither of them felt the need to 'find' that special someone, nor did they feel their value was somehow raised because they were in a relationship. On the other hand, each intermittently went on dates though nothing serious ever evolved. They were devoted to completing the education; their focus was to establish their careers; consequently both got teased a lot.

Their faculties were on very separate parts of the university. So, their paths rarely crossed.

Jordan knew that someday he would find the 'right' gal but was in no hurry. Better to be well established before engaging in something that could distract him. He enjoyed female company and had many female friends. He was a good looking young man and considered a 'hot catch' but no one ever 'caught' him.

Jasmine was a very gentle 'soul'. She was the one everyone went to with all their concerns whether they were academic, relationship, or family issues. Jasmine was the patient understanding one who had the time for everyone, just not for herself. She had a great sense of humor, but only reveled in it with her family and close friends. She was known as a 'quiet gentle beauty,' the kind that focused more on the inner self rather than on the outer characteristics. She knew not to 'judge a book by its cover' and knew that the inner self, or the 'true self' as she referred to it, was always far more important. Her beliefs were regularly reinforced with various good looking guys who chased her then repeatedly turned out to be superficial. The lack of self-development turned her off and left her cold.

Her passion was studying. She loved to study the body and how it functioned; loved to learn how the body healed; and to discover all the different ways the body compensated when things went wrong. Yet there was something missing from all the medical school academia, something she could never put her finger on. It was there, gnawing at her. She thought if she studied hard enough, she would resolve the gnawing, so she studied harder and harder. Her study partner, Galen, was a young woman with a Masters in Herbal Medicine. Galen loved to challenge Western Medicine concepts, hypotheses and claims and so the two of them made great study partners. They loved to find ways to bridge the gap between the two styles of healing.

When Jasmine and Jordon graduated, they moved to the same city to start their practices. Jasmine worked for a general hospital and Jordan worked for a large architect firm as an architectural engineer. He wanted to get good experience under his belt before he ventured out on his own. Ultimately, he wanted his own company.

Although Jordan loved all kinds of architecture, he wanted to focus on housing. His passion was designing unique 'green' homes employing innovation to capture, modify and alter the energies in electricity, heat and water. In his spare time, he relentlessly researched newly developed 'green' systems and modified them to incorporate into novel home designs to expand his portfolio.

He understood responsibility and accountability. He knew he had to develop a marketing and advertising campaign and he needed good solid experience under his belt along with a recognized reputation. He planned to have a significant portfolio when he opened his own office and was prepared to put in the time and effort to achieve it. He knew the time would come, when life was ready. He was a healthy young man and in no need of a physician.

Four years after Jasmine left university, she was well established in a hospital practice. She had more than paid her dues; always working overtime and putting in extra shifts. So, in addition, to being very good at what she did, her movement up the ladder was relatively quick. Now she was thinking of taking her first vacation since her second year as an undergrad. Her family was relieved. They knew how hard she worked and were always concerned she was going to 'burn out' way before her time.

Chapter 3

Jordan Goes to Africa

Jordan was almost ready to go independent. He had everything in order. But he wanted to do a little travelling first. He might not have finances to travel, once he opened his own office. He had no idea where to go. What place in the world would provide him with some novel insights into developing 'Green' homes? He explored online to see if there was anything that reached out to him naturally. Africa kept coming up, but he didn't really want to go to Africa. He was thinking more of some easy European country, not hot difficult Africa.

A program came up asking for volunteers. It was a medical program in Tanzania looking for volunteers to help design a 'Green' hospital. Monies were virtually non-existent, and they needed some way to rely more on solar and earth resources as opposed to the more conventional electricity and hydro power. It not only caught his eye but stayed with him. Eventually he decided to apply – if they said yes, he figured, he was meant to go. If they said no, he would go to Europe.

'Yeah right,' he thought to himself, *'as if they are really going to say no.'* But he wanted to help people and so he went ahead and sent in the application. And of course, they said yes.

His didn't have a family physician, so he went to a clinic and they prescribed the appropriate vaccinations; he applied for a passport; and then went online to see what he should pack and get some helpful travel hints. Before going, he did a lot of research on different methods utilized around the world that would help generate the utilities this hospital required.

He was finally ready to go. He told his parents and family what he was going to do at a family dinner. They all simply raised their eyebrows. He was definitely the outlaw in the family. Everyone else had respectable law degrees and worked for very large firms. They worked long hard hours until they got partnership and secured their futures. Jordan, on the other hand, had to be different. Not only did he go into architecture, but he wanted to create and design things. And if that wasn't bad enough, he had this thing about working with the earth and not abusing it; and of course, he actually wanted to open his own office. His family thought he was a 'flake'. And now, he wanted to go and volunteer in Africa. Nobody needed to say anything, their faces said it all. His dad just shook his head, with an attitude of disgust and changed the conversation.

He wanted not to care. Everyone had always been pretty outspoken about him being the black sheep in the family. He had learned to stop looking for their validation or recognition, long ago. Yet tonight, he was really hoping they might appreciate he could make life better for some others in Africa. He admonished himself for still feeling hurt and disappointed. He knew better. So as usual, he just pushed it down.

It seemed as if in no time at all, he was landing in Africa. The next day he was in a jeep and heading towards somewhere unknown.

His guide took him to meet his Supervisor, Dave. It was in a small community that had no electricity or running water except in the rainy season. Dave sat him down at an outdoor café resembling an old makeshift shanty. The owner brought them out coffee as they talked. Dave showed him what they had: the dimensions of the hospital; the rooms required; the offices and the makeshift bachelor suites for the physicians who would come to volunteer their time. What they needed was unique and novel ways to utilize the resources at hand to create utilities.

Jordan came prepared with some pretty unique and unusual concepts he had found on the internet. He asked Dave if he could see what they were currently working with as it would help them figure out what they could integrate the ideas with the resources at hand. It was one thing to hear their plans, but if they actually saw how and what they were working with, it might provoke some good ideas.

The following day, Dave took Jordan out to the makeshift hospital, complete with a generator and a sagging tarp overhead. Jordan was astounded with what they were working with. Anything would be an improvement. He talked at length with Dr. Simpson and then Dave took him back to the community where they hoped to develop some ingenious ideas. And they did. As they worked, Jordan got more and more excited about the work he was doing. He was creative and ingenious, and the ideas kept pouring forth well into the nights. He would sleep for a few hours, during which time he would dream up some more ideas which he laughingly attributed to Professor Merlin who came into his dreams to provoke creative ideas. In the morning Jordan would be fast at it before Dave even got up.

In no time at all, they had it all working, well at least on paper. Jordan and Dave went into the nearest city to see what resources they could draw on. They approached several different organizations and got the supplies they needed. Everyone was thrilled at the economics of the project.

Jordan already had ideas running around in his head of how he could use this project as a precedent for other projects around the world.

Chapter 4

Jasmine Goes to Africa

Jasmine had a desire to go to foreign lands; meet and understand different cultures; and learn their healing methods. She wanted to spread her wings and travel. She chose to start with Africa, though not too sure why, she just had a gut feeling. She applied to volunteer for the "Doctors without Boundaries" program. She laughed to herself, *'Okay so it really wasn't a vacation in the typical sense of lying on the beach and getting a tan. But it was time away from the hospital while continuing to do her life passion – help heal people.'*

The program readily accepted her. She was leaving in two months, enough time to get her vaccinations and passport organized; have someone take over for her at the hospital; and say goodbye to family and friends. She was going for three months. She was so excited. She exhausted the internet exploring the culture; the agriculture and vegetation; and the native healing remedies. She couldn't wait to go. Her family didn't want her to go. There were too many political problems and she could get sick and what if she were hurt. They had so many reasons to keep her safe at home, but she wasn't having any of it. She wanted outside experience. She wanted to help the world. She went on her service of duty.

When she landed, she felt like she was an old-time traveler. Yet she had never stepped outside the US. In fact, she had never travelled much in the US. But, she felt like she was accustomed to travelling. A strange sensation, but she liked it.

A young African boy held a sign with her name as she came out of the airport in Tanzania. He spoke little English, but enough for the two of them to communicate. He told her she would be staying at a hotel, that night, near the airport. The following day they would travel to the site where she was working. "Actually," he grinned, "it will take a couple of days to get there."

Jasmine was fine with it all. She wanted to have a shower and get cleaned up. She explained to her new 'companion' that she felt like she had a layer of grime on her from all of the travelling.

He laughed, "Wait till you get where we are going," he communicated in his broken English.

She smiled thinking to herself, '*Well, this was the adventure she had been looking for. But had she really taken everything into consideration?*'

He waited for her while she showered and changed her clothes and they went downstairs to have dinner. They had an early night as they apparently wanted to get started while it was still dark and cool. Their travel over the next couple of days provided her with enough information to write a book on.

When they arrived at the 'hospital,' she discovered it was basically a 'lean to' with a tarp covering. She was introduced to the 'head' physician, Dr. Simpson, while he was injecting a small child with a vaccination. He was too busy to stop and take the time to sit down and talk with her. She could see the line ups of people; organized in different lines for different issues. They were obviously short staffed. He told her to wash her hands in the disinfectant 'over there' and she could work with him till she got the 'hang of it'.

By the end of the first day, she was exhausted. She wanted a shower and to lie down on her own bed. Instead she got to have a bit of a sponge bath and a camp bed. It ultimately didn't matter; she was too tired and too hot to look for her nightgown. She slept in her t-shirt and briefs. She fell asleep so fast even the discomfort of the cot didn't matter.

Morning came too fast. She was up and, on her feet, when it was still dark. They had to organize their preparations for the day. Her suitcase was still lying beside her cot as she hadn't had time to unpack.

Maybe tonight.

Chapter 5

Jasmine's Tour of Duty in Africa

She quickly learned Dr. Simpson had been nicknamed 'Hawkeye' from the MASH TV series and she understood why. He had a great sense of humor, similar to MASH's Hawkeye's. And, he was the one everyone turned to when they needed to find a solution to any challenge, again like MASH's Hawkeye.

As they moved from one patient to another, she asked Dr. Simpson about the hospital they were supposed to be in. He explained the hospital was still in the making; there had been a few delays. He told her he'd wondered when she was going to ask. According to the project definition she had applied for, they were already supposed to be in the hospital. The completion wasn't far away, only around the next bend. He told her they had brought in volunteer architects and engineers to create a 'Green' hospital that relied on the earth and the sun for power in creative, ingenious ways.

There was no way the corrupt government was going to provide them with funds to bring the necessary water and electricity way out here even though there were so many people who desperately needed medical care. To resolve this, the program they were working for put out requests to the various communities in North America and Europe asking for volunteers to design, create and build the hospital. It was more than halfway built. Everyone was counting the days till it could open, even for basic clinic care. Unfortunately, the date kept changing.

He explained that when they were through this current shipment of medical care supplies (there was usually a week's break between finishing one shipment of medical care supplies and receiving the next) and if there were no major attacks by the activists during that time; he would take her over to the new hospital to look around. In the meantime, they had a lot of work to accomplish.

Jasmine was surprised at how fast she acclimatized to the heat; the work; the environment; even the food. By the end of the first week, she was considered an 'old pro'. She even started to pick up on the language; bits and pieces became phrases and eventually sentences; but then when you were surrounded by it for 12-16 hours a day; needing to ask questions and needing to understand the answers, what else was there to do?

Chapter 6

Hawkeye Introduces Jordan

At the end of her second week, Hawkeye asked if she wanted to go and see the new 'Green' hospital tomorrow. They required Hawkeye to check in with the project supervisor on a regular basis.

Their current shipment of medical supplies was depleted, and he was making plans to go to the project tomorrow. Jasmine readily agreed. She wanted to see what this "Green' hospital would provide them with. He explained it might take them an hour to get there. She raised an eyebrow, *'So that's what 'just around the bend' means here,'* she said to herself.

They would be leaving before dawn and spending the day there. They would have to take their own water and food as they didn't want to take anything away from the rations provided for the workers.

Busara, a black woman, was Jasmine's designated assistant, and gently woke Jasmine up every morning. But today, Busara woke Jasmine up extra early. She already made Jasmine an oatmeal kind of breakfast, African outback style. She told Jasmine to eat and dress quickly; Hawkeye was almost ready to go. Jasmine dressed and took the bowl and spoon with her to the jeep.

Hawkeye laughed at the bowl in her hand and told her, "Good timing. Let's see if you will actually be able to eat that during the drive." When she raised an eyebrow to his comment, he clarified, "let's just say it is not a smooth American highway and leave it at that." Busara had obviously known what the trip would be like and provided Jasmine with a towel. Jasmine had thought the towel was meant to wipe the perspiration from her forehead but now realized it was to protect her from the flying bits of oatmeal. Hawkeye just laughed.

When they came around the last bend in the makeshift highway, a large ranch style building loomed ahead of them. It certainly wasn't a hospital by any American standards, but it was a large building with a very strange roof and bizarre apparatus along its walls. Hawkeye explained the strange appearances were due to different 'Green' components that had been incorporated into the structure. He further explained to Jasmine there was a very intelligent young architect on site who was particularly interested in incorporating unique designs into the architecture to take advantage of the surrounding aspects of the earth to generate power, light and heat. He had come at the beginning of the project to help design and build the 'Green' hospital. He returned home several months ago but was recognized as a major contributor to the design and effectiveness of the building.

Dave, the supervisor, heard the jeep coming and knew it was Hawkeye. When he came out to greet Hawkeye, and give him the expected tour and report, he was obviously surprised to see Jasmine. "Now that's a sight for sore eyes here in the outback of Africa. Where did you steal this pretty young thing from?" he wanted to know. He was obviously a tease like Hawkeye.

"I'm never telling," responded Hawkeye, "how are you doing, Dave? This is Dr. Jasmine."

"Well isn't this interesting. Jordan just arrived back last night. He wanted to make a couple of adjustments and volunteered to come back for another two months to see how they could incorporate them. Wait till he sets eyes on our Dr. Jasmine here."

As if by design, Jordan walked up at that point and gave Hawkeye a big hug, "Good to see you, old friend."

Hawkeye laughed, "I hear you just couldn't stay away and had to come back to see us again."

Hawkeye introduced Jasmine to Jordan and noticed Jordan's raised eyebrow, "What is a pretty young doctor like you doing out here in the outback of Africa?"

"Well, I guess something similar to what a good looking young architect is doing out here in the outback of Africa," she retorted easily.

There was a moment's silence and then everyone started to laugh, and it was suddenly as if they were all old friends. "Do you have time to tour me around and explain this hospital you have created?" Jasmine asked.

Hawkeye smiled, Jasmine wasn't the shy gentle thing that had arrived on the doorsteps of his hospital camp a few weeks back. Life had changed her quickly; she had grown up fast. No longer the gentle sweet hospital MD from the

US, she was now a confident worldly MD who knew what she wanted and wasn't afraid to ask. He was amazed at how often he had seen the transformation amongst the volunteers sent to him. And now here, it had happened again with Jasmine.

She walked off beside Jordan and Hawkeye wondered if they might connect in another way. After all, they were both about the same age; had both dared to break the safety of their professions by coming out to the outback of Africa; and they both wanted to change in the world. '*It was a possibility*,' he thought to himself and with that he went off with Dave to get the update he had come for.

Jordan was proud of his contributions to the design of the hospital. He was hoping they could use it as a precedence for other places. There were many places around the world needing a hospital service but not able to rely on the country's finances or infrastructure to provide these services, nor the utilities needed. He came to life as he talked to Jasmine about what he had created for the hospital. He explained all the innovations from the roof; to the canals down the side of the building; to how they resourced from the earth itself. It was an amazing creation. She loved the passion he had for his work and enjoyed listening to him. She didn't quite understand everything he was explaining, but she got the general concepts.

Her passion for her work crosslinked with his passion for construction; she was so excited about how this hospital. How it would make their work so much easier than what they were doing under the UN tarps. Just the hygiene alone was going to be a vast improvement, never mind having to rely on a generator that was constantly breaking down.

After he showed her the emergency room; the pharmaceutical lab; the small operating facility; and the facility for vaccinations; he showed her the physicians' offices. She was delighted with everything and laughed when he showed her the small bachelor suites attached to the physicians' offices. They would share a bathroom between every two and they would only have their camp cots to begin with. But down the road, they hoped to bring in proper beds. They would also share a bachelor kitchen with a small stove, a fridge, a sink and counter. Jasmine was so excited. She explained to Jordan the makeshift camp they were working out of now and how she had a makeshift cot and a sheet to give her privacy. This was like going from a tent to the Taj Mahal in India.

He smiled with pleasure at her enthusiasm. He already knew of the camp where she was working. He had been there when he first came to Africa. He had wanted to see what they were currently doing and what their needs were. He was impressed that a pretty young doctor like herself was willing to leave the safety and comfort of a hospital in the US to come and work out of a makeshift camp like they had here.

When he finished the tour, he asked if she wanted to come over to the canteen for lunch, where they could sit and talk. She explained Hawkeye had organized for them to bring their own water and food, so they didn't take from the workers' rations at the hospital. Jordan knew everyone was rationed, so he didn't argue. They walked over to Hawkeye's jeep and collected her lunch and then walked over to the canteen to collect his. They sat and talked over lunch sharing their work and their passions.

When Hawkeye and Dave finished their rounds, they walked into the canteen. Hawkeye noticed them right away. He motioned to Dave to take a look at the two of them talking. They were both animated. There was definitely a spark going on between them.

Hawkeye asked Dave if there was any reason or excuse to send Jordan over to their camp in the next few weeks so the two of them could get together again. Dave smiled; he didn't know Hawkeye was such a match maker. This land and this work just didn't lend a hand to much of that. This was all the more reason to take advantage of the opportunity that laid itself open to them. Dave promised to figure something out. Hawkeye explained to Dave there wasn't much to do for the next week until the new shipment came in. It was a great time to organize some meetings between the two of them.

Over the next few weeks, Jasmine and Jordan hit it off incredibly well. They spent hours on end talking about everything from their histories and families; how and why they chose the same university; their university experiences; and how they managed to have missed each other so many times. How weird it was they had both moved to the same city to start their practices and again missed each other so many times. The best part was that it took them coming to Africa to actually meet. What were the odds of that?

The conversations went on to embrace philosophies and world religions; to healing modalities around the world; to architecture and new designs to embrace natural resources for utilities around the world. They couldn't get enough of one another; then all of a sudden it was over. Jordan had to go back to the US and Jasmine was here for another two months. But they promised to get to together when Jasmine returned home. He knew the hospital where she worked and promised to come and see her when she returned.

When he was gone, Jasmine felt so alone. He had given color and life to the work she was doing in the makeshift hospital. Now, without him, it was drab. She still loved the fact she could help so many, but it was now black and white rather than full of color. Before, she wasn't anxious to get home. Now she was. *'Damn him anyways,'* she said to herself. Unknowingly she had said it out loud.

"I beg your pardon, Jasmine," Hawkeye responded, "who exactly are you damning, way out here?"

She was embarrassed she had said it out loud and even more embarrassed Hawkeye had been the one that heard her. "Oh, just thinking to myself," she tried to cover up, but Hawkeye wasn't letting her get away with it.

"I have a sneaky suspicion the color has gone out of your experience here since Jordan went back home," he said with a smug smile and a raised eyebrow.

"Oh geez, is it that obvious!" now Jasmine was really embarrassed.

"Well, I wouldn't say it is that obvious to everyone. But old matchmaker here was watching how the two of you hit it off from the moment you met. You each brought out the passion in the other. It was great to see. You two could make a great team, going around and saving the world, each with your own talents. I wish I had a partner like that to travel from one project to another with. You are lucky. You shouldn't let that opportunity get away. I hope the two of you are planning to connect when you get back home."

Jasmine went red with embarrassment. It was like he had read her thoughts. Was she really that transparent? She had even dreamt of Jordan since he had left and doing the very things Hawkeye had suggested. She hadn't said a word before Hawkeye started again.

"I can see I have 'hit the nail on the head'." he said with pleasure, "Have the two of you organized when and how you will continue with this romance back home?" He pushed for more information.

"Well, not really. I mean it's not a romance. All we've done is talk. We've never even kissed," she paused for a moment. Should she say anything more? "He knows when I am returning, and he knows the hospital I work in. He said he will come to the hospital and we will go from there; nothing definite or specific." she admitted.

"From what I saw between the two of you, he will follow through. I am sure of that." Hawkeye didn't let her off the hook for the next two months. He teased her whenever and however he could. She was getting a thick skin on that level and started to shovel back what he handed out. It made for a great working relationship. There was a lot of fun and laughter which was desperately needed in a place like this.

Chapter 7

Now That's a Greeting

Jasmine returned home a week ago. Her family had all met her at the airport. They were surprised she was fit and in good health. Her mother was close to tears, with relief.

It was now over a week and she had not heard from Jordan. She had been longing to see him again. Now she was trying to come to terms that he obviously was not as taken with her as she had been with him. Her heart was broken. She attempted to focus on her work to get her mind off him. But it was difficult. She had spent the last six weeks recalling every conversation they had shared, every word they had exchanged. She had dreamt up all kinds of different scenarios for how he might welcome her home or meet her at the hospital. All were in vain. This just reinforced why she never got involved. Who wanted to go through this kind of heartbreak? They had never even slept together. She couldn't imagine what it would have been like if she had actually slept with him.

She cried herself to sleep the last two nights. She felt drained and exhausted, more so now than she had felt when she returned home from doing three months of duty out under the sun or under the canvas tarp. She woke up in the morning dragging her feet. Her passion for her work seemed to have been sucked right out of her. She did her morning hygiene routine, got dressed and went to work feeling sad and alone.

There he was standing outside of her office with balloons that said "Welcome Home" and a beautiful bouquet of flowers. They weren't just flowers, they were orchids. She had told him somewhere along the line, her favorite flowers were orchids. He had heard, and he had remembered. Her heart burst with excitement and then anger and then hurt. She wasn't sure what to stick with.

"You're a little late, aren't you?" she asked, trying to keep all emotion from her voice.

"Yes, you are right. I had a family emergency and had to fly back home. My dad had a heart attack and was in the hospital. I didn't have any other contact information to get hold of you and the hospital didn't know me from Adam, so when I asked for your number they refused to give it. I am so sorry. I just got back into town late last night. I came to the hospital, but you had already gone home. They said you started today at 8AM so I have been here since 7:30 hoping you might come in early."

Well how could she be angry with all that? The anger and hurt dropped away and she ran up to him and gave him a big hug. "Thank you for being here. I was so looking forward to seeing you again. How is your dad?" the doctor in her heard heard and was concerned about the heart attack and had to know how his father was. She had moved to let go. She was embarrassed she had ran up to hug him. But he wouldn't let her go.

"Now this feels good," he smiled at her.

She motioned for him to let her go so she could open the door to her office. She didn't want others to see them hugging in the hallway. Everyone knew she didn't have boyfriends and this was going to cause a commotion of questions and teasing. He let her go and moved to the side, so she could unlock her office door. They moved inside her office and he closed the door behind him.

"Now can we finish that hug? I have never had a hug that felt so good." He turned her around to face him. She had a big smile on his face and he knew his emotions were returned. He took a leap of faith and bent down to kiss her. She returned his kiss as well.

'*God this has to be the one,*' he said to himself. He finally let go of her as he took a moment to catch his breath. "Have you got time to talk before you start? Can I take you to breakfast? I have been dying to see you again. That doesn't sound very macho, does it? I am not supposed to be showing you my vulnerable side, at least not at this stage of our relationship. I seem to have lost all my pride with you."

She beamed. It was so good to know he felt the same way she did. She wanted to take the day and just go celebrate with him. It was worth the wait, maybe even the hurt. This was just such a good emotional place to be. She asked him what his schedule was like for the day. He told her he had booked the morning off, but he could probably get the whole day off. He said it as a question, '*God, if she could get the day off too,*' he would be in 7th heaven. He didn't say it out loud; he knew he already sounded like some love sick teenager. She smiled with that upside down grin he loved so much.

"Let me see if I can get some time off," she phoned her supervisor and explained a colleague had unexpectedly come in from Africa and was there any chance she could get the day off. She apologized for it being such late notice, but he had just arrived. Her supervisor knew Jasmine had never been late; had never asked for time off except for the African project, which actually made for good advertising for the hospital. So she told Jasmine to take the day off and go enjoy it with the colleague. Jasmine got off the phone and struggled not to give it away. She couldn't stop smiling and Jordan knew she got the break.

"How long?" he asked.

"The whole day," she was going to get a sore jaw if she didn't stop smiling from ear to ear. "Let's go figure out what we are going to do with it," she said as she guided him back out the door. He put an arm around her shoulders as they walked down the hallway and out the door.

She wasn't unaware of all the nurses' looks and raised eyebrows. Between the balloons and the orchids and the arm around her shoulders, not to mention the good-looking guy walking beside her, she knew tomorrow was going to be a day to reckon with. But today, today, she didn't care.

"How far do you live from here?" he wanted to know, "we could take these flowers and balloons back to your place and find a vase with some water. I can get a sneak look at your apartment and then we could go out for breakfast and figure out what we are going to do for the rest of the day," he suggested.

She was still grinning from ear to ear. Why would she have any issue with such a great plan? Sure; of course; why not; and sounds great. What was she supposed to say when she was 'flying on cloud nine'?

They dropped off his gifts and he looked around the apartment while she found a vase and filled it with water.

"This place doesn't suite you, you know? It is too austere, and you are too full of life. But right now, I really don't care. Let's go for breakfast."

Chapter 8

A Special Home

The skies were dark and heavy and the air felt like it was going to snow. Juliana ran back into their barraca. She took off the layers of clothes wrapping her body, protecting her from the cold as she collected wood for the fire.

She had a young one lying in a bundle beside the fire. She checked on her; '*Yup, still sleeping soundly.*'

Jordian had built a stone fireplace in the middle of the barraca styled home he had built for them. He had travelled far in his youth and explored all kinds of different homes. He fell in love with the barraca homes he saw in the south.

Way back when, when they got together, he built them a very different home from the ones in the community. Being forever the creative one, he made improvements upon the different barraca he had seen in his earlier travels. Their home was very unique. When they came to the community, they made friends quickly and easily, and many came to help Jordian build their home.

She remembered the two of them laughing about whether their new friends and neighbors came to help and be neighborly; whether they came to make friendly with the new healer in town; or whether they came to figure out 'what the hay' Jordian was building. They decided it was probably some combination of all three for everyone.

Jordian was very creative with everything he did. The fireplace, built in the center of the house, warmed tunnels of water providing heated floors throughout the house. It was built in a similar fashion to the hypocausts from the Roman era that allowed for a form of central heating. He built a beautiful container on the roof that collected water and channeled it down a pathway alongside the stone fireplace allowing the water to heat as it moved into the house.

Juliana was creative as well, but in very different ways. She was an herbalist and a healer for the community. She collected various gems and crystals along with plants and herbs to make her special healing concoctions.

Jordian was very proud of the healing work Juliana did. People would travel for weeks on end to bring her their loved ones who were suffering. She was known for being able to heal everyone and anything.

When they were building the barraca, he talked with her about what she might need down the road, so he could incorporate it into the design of their home. He created a special channel down one side of the fireplace. Into the channel he created little shelves where she could place gems and crystals which provoked the water to dance down the channel like they did in a waterfall. The shelves had little one way doors on them preventing the water from coming out into the home, but allowing Juliana to change the gems and crystals as necessary. Juliana was thrilled. She knew the power of water. She knew water had a memory of sorts as it moved and danced; it had a capacity to create special patterns in accordance to its surroundings. She could see how the energy of the water changed in accordance to what she laid on those shelves. It added a special component to her healing abilities.

Jordian was pleased he had talked with her before designing their home. It had taught him a valuable lesson. Always listen to what a person needs and never assume you know their needs before designing something for them. Since that time, Jordian often assisted Juliana with her work. He watched how she used the special waters and changed their vibrational frequencies with the various crystals and gems and herbs. Part of what made Juliana so good with her healing arts was that she had the capacity to see the energies. She could see energy around people and around the plants and herbs she used. She knew with her sixth sense what went together and what didn't.

Today she had gone out to collect some wood for the fireplace and to attend to one of her 'special gardens.' Although she had five 'special gardens' and her own regular vegetable garden, they each required a different type of attention; either with different cycles of the moon or with different times of the year. This had all become second nature to her over the years. She was good at growing what her family needed and what her clients needed and was always very careful to protect the seeds from each plant, so she could continue to grow them from one season to the next. Her general garden was laid out behind the barraca. It provided a place to grow all the general herbs and spices, fruits and vegetables for her family's day to day needs. She not only knew the different types and times for harvesting but was good at preparing the foods in the different ways to keep them through the cold of winter.

Jordian also created five 'special gardens' for Juliana. In one garden she grew the plants and herbs and spices that were seasonal and provided greater medicinal components for her clients.

The second 'special garden' was in a special darkened room she and Jordian had designed for the primary purpose of fungus and mushrooms that loved the dark. She grew over 100 different types of mushrooms. They were so good for a number of medicinal issues. There were also special mosses and other plants that loved the dark as well.

The third 'special garden' was above the barraca. Again, Jordian had worked with to her to develop this 'special garden'. It needed more concentrated sunlight for those plants that grew in more tropical areas. She, and her Master Herbalist, travelled far to get these special plants and prepare the seeds for travel. Since, they required more heat around the year, Jordian had incorporated the use of the fireplace to generate more heat in this 'special garden'. The roof of the garden was made of distinct plant leaves prepared with an oil that drew in the sun's light and helped to create a 'hot house' effect.

The fourth garden was a raised garden off the ground for plants liking wet soggy kinds of soils. It was designed to have poor drainage to keep the soils damp. It was positioned under a tree with heavy thick leaves, to keep the sun from drying out the soils in the hotter times of the year.

The final garden was for plants that liked hot dry soils, more like the soils of a desert her Mentor had told her about, but she had never seen.

Over time, Jordian's creative unique designs earned him a reputation. At the same time, Juliana's gardens and healing capacity earned her a reputation.

Individually, they were held in very high esteem. Together they made an awesome couple.

Chapter 9

Merlin

Juliana studied under a great Herbal Master in her youth. She had been with him ever since her woman characteristics started developing. He was always very good to her. He was considered THE Master Herbalist of his time.

At one point, he had taken her to a special waterfall. They had travelled many moons to get to the waterfalls. He had told her to be patient, it was worth the travel. He explained that as the water jumped and leaped over the falls, it changed its form. As the water cleansed itself; changed its form; it became a potent base for healing.

Juliana never forgot the days she spent with her Herbal Master. She was very fortunate to have spent several years under his guidance. He was well into his eighties when he crossed over but had shared his magic and healing like a Merlin. So, she nicknamed him 'Merlin'.

She was his last student of that lifetime and he wanted to make sure all the great healing practices would not be lost when he died. So, he spent special time with Juliana, teaching, guiding and training her. When he had finished with her, he laid on his bed and held her hand as he prepared to cross over, "you are my life's delight," he told her, as he squeezed her hand. "You have a natural gift for identifying all the different plants and their varying species and knowing what to do with what. While I shared the wisdom, I gained through the ages with you, you came into this life with your own magical understanding. You have had other masters in other lifetimes. One does not come into a lifetime with a gift such as yours, without prior training."

He closed eyes and paused to catch his dying breaths before continuing, "be careful throughout your life Juliana. There will be those who try to take advantage of you; those who will be jealous and envious of you and negate you. But there will also be those who admire, acknowledge and appreciate your understanding, your wisdom and your capacity to heal. Learn to differentiate between them, so no one is capable of doing you harm," Merlin paused again, to collect his thoughts. He had a lot left to share with Juliana before he crossed over.

"In my dreams, I have seen a man. He is a young, strong, creative man. You will marry him. He will take you away to another place. But he will benefit your work and you will benefit him," her Merlin paused again. She knew he was going. He had known in advance how and when he would cross over. He had no fears or apprehensions; he had seen this too in his dreams over the years. He had taken the time to share his dreams with her, so she too would be prepared when the time came. Taking a deep slow breath, he started again.

"This man is a good man and he will give you three healthy children. There is a very deep special love between you; a love that crosses time."

"How will I know this man, you speak of Merlin?" she wanted to know.

"You will know, my dear, without a shadow of a doubt. You have been together before and the love you share is strong; a sacred love crossing over time; a love that is able to withstand many hardships; it only grows stronger, it never weakens. You are special, my dear. Not too many ever get to share this kind of love. Hold it dear to your heart," he paused again.

"Can I get you some water, My Merlin?" she didn't want to let him go. He had been her mentor and her best friend. She had sat at his feet learning for almost, as long as, she could remember.

"No, My Dear, but thank you. It is close. I see the light. Be strong. I will always be with you; even on the other side. You can draw on me whenever you need, My Blessed Child." He paused again, he had a peaceful smile. He was prepared to cross. He had been working at a spiritual level for many moons to prepare for this event. He was a 'cross over'. There were not many like him anymore; those who knew how to cross over between this dimension and the other dimensions.

Her 'Merlin' had taken much time with her teaching. He had even taught her what it would be like when she learned to be a 'cross over'. He had explained she would not develop the capacity until after her third child, but he wanted her to understand as much as she could about it now, when he was still with her.

She was losing him; her friend, her mentor, her travel companion. What would she ever do without him? He could see the thoughts running through her mind. "Not to worry, my dear. I will be there with you wherever you go. I will never abandon you, whether I am on this side or the other. We still have much to accomplish."

"I know you are ready to go and I want to be able to let you go so you can continue your journey. I really do. But there is such a big part of me that wants to hang on. When I left my parents, there was you. Now you are leaving, and I have no-one," she shared her concern and apprehension with him.

"Remember, My Child, when you start your journey as a 'cross over' you will see me again. In the meantime, you will feel me with your heart and your sixth sense. You will know I am with you."

"Yes, yes, you keep telling me that. I believe you. I am still finding it hard to let go. How do I do that?"

"It is part of learning acceptance, My Child; accepting the web and flow of life, the comings and goings of souls. Acceptance is a huge part of truly growing up and developing as a human being. Many people grow old, but few people grow up. Many who think they have grown up have no idea what it entails. They get caught up in delusional beliefs that stunt their growth. Learn to put your time and energy into that which you can change. Learn to know that which you do not have the power to change and let it go. Do not waste your time trying to change something you cannot; whether that be a person, an event, or life itself. Many people waste a lifetime struggling to change things which they cannot or resisting things they have no power against. Remember what I have taught you: set your plans; organize your course; then let life take you where it may.

You will have many choices to make in life; but there are a few choices you have already made before you came into this life. We make those kinds of choices at a much higher soul level. The choice we have here is whether we will engage in those choices we have set out for ourselves before we entered this world. If we waste our life trying to change things we cannot, then we waste the time we have to engage in those things we can change; to learn the lessons we have the opportunity to learn; and to develop the relationships we have the time to develop.

The lesson here at this time is learning to accept and let go. When we learn that lesson in the way we are meant to, there is really no need for grieving. We grieve when we refuse to let go. And we hang on, but to what? Love both the self and me enough to accept and let go." And with that, he squeezed her hand one more time, smiled that smile she had loved so much throughout her training. That smile that told her she had done well. With that smile, he crossed over to the other side and his body was gone.

She let a tear fall and then put into practice all he had given her about acceptance. She stood up and walked out of the little abode they had built for him to cross over in. She went down to the Danube River, which ran through the countryside and alongside the abode, and sat down. She closed her eyes and focused on her Merlin. She went deep into that inner place he had taught her to go. She could go there easily now and in moments found herself outside her body and up in the 'astral' realms with Merlin. She could see he no longer had his earthly body but was a colorful pattern of energy. She felt his smile surround her and his paternal love penetrate every aspect of her being.

She was good now. She could let him go. She opened her eyes again and was down by the riverside. She felt a peace and acceptance flow through her being and she smiled up in gratitude. Even in his crossing over, he had taught her another lesson.

Chapter 10

Two Men

After Juliana's time with her 'Merlin' was over, she didn't know what to do with herself. He had taught her so much she was so appreciative of; he had left with so many special seeds from around the world she was grateful for; but now what was she going do with her day to day living.

'Merlin' told her she was to pack her things and go south. She was going to meet her beloved on a pathway leading south. He wasn't sure when, or how, but knew it was on a pathway going south. So, she organized all of her things; put her belongings on one horse and rode the other. South; what did that mean; how far south? Was she supposed to go more southeast or more southwest? *Why didn't she get more clarification before Merlin crossed over?* she moaned to herself.

And then she heard a voice; it was Merlin. She stopped the horses. One of them pawed the ground and she told it to be quiet. She listened, "Merlin, is that you? Are you telling me which way to go?" she listened again.

There was nothing, just the silence of the woods. She jumped down from the horse and waited and waited, hoping to hear his voice. And then, she felt a hand push her shoulder forward. "Is that you Merlin? Please talk to me?" she begged.

After a while, she got back up on her horse and started again. Now she was intent on hearing, feeling, and working with any sense that would give her guidance from her Merlin.

She came to a fork in the road, "Okay Merlin, please tell me which way to go?" she pleaded. Both horses held their ears high; they were hearing something. *'Could they hear Merlin?'* she wondered to herself, not wanting to break the silence in case she missed Merlin. And the horses moved forward and took the path to the right without her lead. She allowed them to move, hoping it was Merlin guiding them.

And then she heard the voice again, "Well done, My Child. Learn to follow your senses," Merlin whispered to her in the ethereal plane. She was so excited. She wanted to talk with him, but he remained elusive to her. Yet, at each step along the way, he guided her in some way.

They continued on for a couple of weeks. Travelling and resting; gathering wood for a fire and food to cook in the evenings. "Was she ever going to find what she was looking for? Really, what was it she was looking for?" she asked to the skies one night. They did not answer; millions of eyes simply watched her.

Merlin came to her that night in her dreams. He told her the next day was going to be very special. She needed to pay attention, "To what?" she asked.

"Just pay attention and you will know," was all he would tell her.

The following morning, she woke up excited. What was it she was going to find or see or hear today? She couldn't wait to get going. The horses seemed excited too, as if they knew something was going to happen today as well. They moved along the trails throughout the morning and saw nothing except a large group of rabbits. Great for eating but surely that wasn't what her Merlin had told her to watch out for. It was mid to late afternoon when she heard it. It was another horse coming down the path towards her. She looked up to the sky as if to ask Merlin, "Was this what she was supposed to be attending to?"

He came through the forest. He was a tall man and appeared to be alone. He stopped when he saw her, "And what do we have here? A maiden in distress?" he queried.

"I am not in distress sir," she responded, "I am simply making my way south. I am on a mission."

"Oh, and what kind of a mission would take a young lady through the woods?" he sneered at her.

She didn't like his tone or his expression. Was this what Merlin was telling her to be attentive to? She tried to move past him, but he made it difficult for her. She asked him to kindly let her pass, so she could be on her way. He was not interested in giving her the way she asked for. He blocked her horse and grabbed one of her bags; one of the bags with the precious seeds.

"Let's see what we have here," and he opened the bag and spilled the contents.

Juliana tried not to show her anger, or her fear, and instead said with a tone of attitude and determination, "That was not a kind thing to do, Sir. Please let me move on." She wanted him to go away. She needed to get off her horse and pick up her seeds. But she didn't want him to know how precious they were to her. She was shaking inside and sending up prayers to Merlin to please help.

Another man rode into view. '*Oh no,*' she thought, '*not another one. Can't you please leave me alone?*' she pleaded silently.

The second man rode up to her horse and asked what the meeting was about. The first man told the second she was his and he was just having a little trouble getting his woman into line.

"I am not your woman!" Juliana exclaimed, "You are a brute and you are rude and you have dumped my seeds all over the ground." She hadn't wanted to let them know how precious her seeds were. But the fact he had claimed her to be his own had overruled her thoughts and she let out her secret.

The second man got off his horse. He walked over to Juliana and asked if she were telling the truth.

"Of course, I am." she exclaimed indignantly, "I never tell a lie. And how dare you lie about me." she directed at the first man.

"Well then," the second man said to the first, "perhaps we shall be on our way?" he directed the first man with a definite air of confidence. "I will stay and help the young maiden pick up her seeds."

The first man obviously recognized the younger man was bigger and more fit than he and was not willing to put up a fight. And so, with an obscenity, he galloped off leaving the two behind in the woods.

"What are these seeds that they are so important?" the second man asked of Juliana.

"They are special seeds that help me grow what I need to heal people of their ailments," she shared with the man and then asked herself, '*Now why did I tell him that?*'

"And where are you headed with your precious seeds that help people heal?" he gently pushed for more information.

"I am going south." she offered and asked herself why he got to ask all of the questions, "And where are you headed, kind sir?"

"I am headed in the opposite direction, I am headed north. What kind of mission would take a young lady south, may I ask?"

"I am not entirely sure, kind sir. I only know my mentor and teacher told me to go south. And I was to pay attention."

"Well, if you don't know what you are looking for or where you are going, perhaps you would like to take a meal with me? Maybe we can figure it out," he offered.

"I would appreciate that. Perhaps you can tell me from whence you have come, so I might know what lies ahead of me."

He tethered his horse and then tethered her two horses before helping her collect her seeds. She noticed the horses didn't seem to mind one another. She, on the other hand, was finding it difficult to locate her seeds as the darkness of the evening began to spread through the trees.

Without having to ask one another, they began to gather wood for a fire and food for a meal. They shared their names and talked easily and worked together as a team without having to ask or direct. Instead their conversation moved about other things; from whence they had come; where they were going; what their purpose and intents were. By the time their meal was ready their camaraderie was easy, it was like they were old friends. The meal and conversation took them into the night. As they fed their horses, they agreed to make their beds there that night.

It was late in the night, when Jordian shared he had been told in a dream he needed to go north. Juliana laughed, saying that was funny, her mentor had told her to go south.

"What are you supposed to find, when you go north?" she asked.

"I am supposed to find My Lady. I will spend a lifetime with her and we will be a good match. We will work well together, and we will love each other deeply. We will have three healthy children between us." He shared.

Juliana didn't say anything. Was this the man Merlin had directed her towards? How could she be sure? It all seemed too easy.

Jordian was waiting for Juliana's response. What was she going south for? She didn't want to share her secret. What if he was the one? She didn't want to seem forward. When he asked again, she told him she would tell him in the morning. Perhaps, Merlin would come to her in the night and let her know what to do.

Eventually, they laid the fire low and rested in their blankets. It was strange to have a man nearby, especially when it wasn't her Merlin. Yet, at the same time there was a comfort about it. She went off to sleep expecting Merlin to come to her.

Chapter 11

A Love That Crosses Time

When she woke in the morning, she was frustrated. Merlin had not come. What was she supposed to do? Would the two of them simply get up and continue on their paths? Was he the man she was supposed to spend a life with? She certainly had liked talking with him the night before and he had certainly saved her from the horrible man. She enjoyed his company and felt at ease with him. They worked well together when they collected their wood for the fire and their food for their evening meal. What was she supposed to do?

She rolled over and looked to see if Jordian was awake. He was gone from his blankets but obviously had not left the area. His blankets were rolled up and his horse was standing next to hers. She sat up and was embarrassed to see him sitting across the fire watching her.

"How long have you been watching me?" she asked with embarrassment and a hint of annoyance.

"No need to get angry Juliana," I am watching you because of a dream I had last night.

Her anger dropped, he had her attention, "A dream? What kind of dream?"

"I told you before, I was told to travel north to find My Lady. Last night I dreamt I had found her. I would like to believe Juliana, you are one I was searching for," he paused letting her take in what he had said.

Juliana was beaming inside. So, he was the one. She hadn't told him last night why she was travelling south. Maybe she would share with him now. He had certainly made himself vulnerable by sharing his dream of the night with her. Maybe it was Merlin who had come to him. She was struggling not to smile and give herself away. She wanted to run over and hug him in delight.

Instead she said with caution, "That is an interesting dream you had, Jordian. Why would you think we should believe a dream that came to you in the night?"

"In the dream, a wise old man told me to tell you, Merlin says 'Well done. It is a love that crosses time'. I am not sure who Merlin is, but I think you know."

"Aye." she said. She had to think through what her next words should be. So, Merlin went to him OR someone went to him and told him about her Merlin. *Had she mentioned Merlin to him last night?* she struggled to quickly review the conversation they had but didn't remember mentioning Merlin.

Jordian was waiting patiently for her. He saw various expressions dance across her face. He knew this was big information for her. It was big for him too. He had been guided to this place; the two of them had worked so well together last night; and had talked as if they were old friends. He was confident this was the one. He wanted her to be just as confident.

Juliana started to talk a few times and then shut her mouth. Merlin had also told her to proceed cautiously.

Finally, she came upon a decision, "If you are correct Jordian, and if you are telling me the truth about your dream and what Merlin says; then I think we should travel for a while together and see what happens and if we are given any further direction." she offered slowly.

"This sounds like a good plan. However, first I want to know what you were going to tell me in the morning."

Oh, she didn't want to tell him, not just yet. And then she felt a push on her shoulder like the one she had felt many days ago. She felt sure it was Merlin. She paused again as she was not sure if she wanted to reveal her secret yet. The push came again. "Okay then, I will." she said to Merlin but there was only Jordian to hear her.

"You will tell me?" he questioned. It seemed to Jordian that she were talking to someone else, but no one else was there.

She sat up straight. She was now sure, "Yes, I will tell you. You see, my mentor and teacher and best friend was Merlin. I was with him for many years. He crossed over recently. But before he crossed over, he told that I was to travel south and along the way I would meet the man I was destined for. He told me in a dream, night before last, that I was to pay attention yesterday, but he did not tell me what to pay attention to. I did not know if I was to pay attention in order to protect myself from that horrible man; or if perhaps I was to pay attention to you."

"And did this Merlin of yours, ever tell you anything about this man you were destined for?" Jordian wanted to know.

"Well yes. He did. He told me that," she paused trying to remember Merlin's exact words, "this man is a good man and he will give you three healthy children. There is a very deep special love between you; a love that crosses time."

"Ahhh, 'three children' and 'a love that crosses time;' this is what the Merlin, in my dream last night, said to me. I have found you, you are the one," Jordian jumped up and danced in a circle. He was so pleased. She was such a desirable thing. And, they got along so well.

He danced over to Juliana and reached down to pull her up into his dance. They danced around the fire and around the horses. '*They even danced well together,*' she thought to herself.

When Jordian had finished dancing, he said they must celebrate with a good breakfast. She laughed in agreement. She collected wood for the fire and he caught a rabbit. She could not bear to see an animal hurt and so she focused on collecting the remainder of her seeds, while he prepared the rabbit. It was much easier finding the fallen seeds in the daylight. She was so pleased with finding her man, that looking for the seeds was now a delight.

Jordian prepared their breakfast and handed her a leaf with a good portion on it. While they ate, she had to ask, "So what is next? What do we do? Where do we go? Where do we live?"

"You are full of questions I do not know the answers to. But I do know of a place not too many days from here. It will provide us with good cover and a place to make plans while we eat and sleep and get to know one another. I would suggest we go there and wait for further direction. We obviously both suffer from another telling us what to do. But if they have led me to you, and you to me, then I must appreciate all the direction they have given us."

Juliana didn't say anything. She simply ate her breakfast and pondered the information he had given her. It was logical; it was pragmatic; and it had a very romantic feel for her. She loved the cross between romance and pragmatics. So, she simply said, "Sounds like a plan."

Chapter 12

Waiting for Direction

They rode for several days before they came to the place Jordian had talked about. It was a small community and he seemed to know most everyone. He had obviously past through this way before.

They were led to a cottage that certainly provided a roof over their head; a place to lie down; and what they needed to prepare meals while they waited for further direction.

In addition, the community provided them a place to get to know one another and to also know one another in the context of other people. It was a good place for them to wait.

While they waited patiently, they shared with one another their histories and their passions. She shared her time with Merlin and all the things he had taught her about how to use plants and herbs and foods to help people heal; how he had taught her to know the difference between witchcraft and folklore magic versus REAL medicine; had trained her to use the sixth sense and her capacity for seeing energies to understand what was wrong with a client and what they needed to restore their health.

She shared with Jordian, the travels she and Merlin had taken to see and understand so many different aspects of nature that were healing, from the waterfalls to the caves where special mosses grew. She even shared with Jordian how Merlin had taught her to go outside herself and between the different life planes.

In return, Jordian shared with her his travels; his love of how different communities built their different abodes and the special ways each utilized nature to their own benefit. He drew diagrams in the sand helping her to understand what he had seen and ideas he had developed.

Eventually, their patience paid off. One night, Merlin came to both of them in their dreams. He told them each they were learning well about one another and he was pleased. Now it was time to move on.

He guided Jordian to the place they were to build their home. He instructed Juliana what to do with her seeds. He instructed both that when their home was built, they were to become one.

Both Juliana and Jordian woke in the morning with excitement; both wanting to tell the other what Merlin had said. Juliana didn't know if she was more excited that she had spent time with her Merlin or more excited about the message he had given her. It was the best night in a long time.

During their time together, and with all that Juliana had shared about her Merlin, Jordian had come to have great respect for her master and was willing to abide by his guidance. He wanted to bed Juliana and it was getting harder and harder to resist. But out of respect for Merlin and out of honor for Juliana, he pushed his need down though it was getting more and more difficult each day.

They packed and organized their belongings and Juliana's seeds that day; made sure their horses were well fed, watered and groomed for the journey. They said their goodbyes to all the friends they had made and set off on their journey.

When Juliana had learned Merlin had guided Jordian to the place they were to build their home, she had complete faith. She followed Jordian without question. She had come to trust Jordian as she already trusted Merlin, so there was no need to question where they were going or how they were going to get there. It was a good feeling to simply follow with the knowingness that it was right.

Chapter 13

A Special Day

Jordan and Jasmine sat in a local restaurant and ate a large breakfast, the first of their celebratory meals. They kept comparing how different this was from Africa; real food; real coffee; real furniture.

By the time their meal was delivered, they started to toss ideas around for things to do for the rest of the day: a walk in the park or down by the river; did she want to see his place; where would they like to go for lunch; for dinner? They had 1001 plans to take in.

"If we do everything, I won't be going back to work for a week," she laughed.

"Okay, well I only have today too. I have to go back to work tomorrow. But, we have future evenings and weekends to take advantage of too. We really could take advantage of everything there is to do in Boston. Are you still doing shift work, do we need to work around that?" his question was simply a question. There wasn't any complaint in it. He was willing to do whatever was necessary. She just had to let him know what he had to deal with and he would.

They spent the rest of the day laughing and joking, hugging and kissing. They couldn't get enough of one another. She wanted to know when the hospital would be complete. He explained they were a little behind schedule. He had ordered special parts, but they hadn't been delivered yet which brought him to another point.

"It should be finished in three weeks. Do you want to come back with me for the ribbon cutting?"

"You are going all the way back there to cut a ribbon?"

"Well, because I designed a number of factors in the hospital, they asked if I would come back for the ribbon cutting and I agreed. But it would be even better if you came with me?"

"I don't think my supervisor will give me more time off. I barely got back from a three-month stint. But I will ask. It would be fun, and I would be able to see Hawkeye again."

They ended up at his place for dinner and ordered in Chinese food. It was something they had both laughed at in Africa: no Chinese food delivery.

She liked his place and unlike hers, his really suited him. Perhaps because he was an architect he was more focused on his home and surroundings. For her, her home had simply been somewhere to rest her head.

They turned on a movie after dinner but couldn't stop talking and ended up turning it off. There was just so much life to talk about. They had gone through two bottles of wine and were both getting a little giddy. Neither of them were normally drinkers.

She looked at her watch, it was already 10PM. They had spent the entire day together. She had never done that with anybody else. Well, that wasn't true. She spent entire days with him when they were in Africa.

She got up to stretch and say she had to go home. She really didn't want to go although she couldn't tell him that, but she did have to get up and actually go to work in the morning.

He didn't want her to go, but could he tell her that? Was it too quick to ask her to stay for the night? God, he sure wanted her too. But he didn't want to push her either.

"You know we have drunk two bottles of wine. You are a doctor and you know what that much alcohol can to someone especially when they are not used to drinking. I think, Dr. Jasmine, you really should stay the night."

"What and sleep on your couch?" she knew what he was really suggesting, but she wanted him to be more direct and not passive-aggressive.

"Well, actually, Dr. Jasmine, I do believe my bed is big enough for two. And, quite frankly, I would like to share more than my bed with you. But I don't want to push you." As he spoke, he got up and walked towards her and pulled her into his arms. His last words were spoken against her lips and he conveyed more effectively what he really wanted, with his mouth.

She returned his kiss giving him the answer he was looking for. They moved down the hallway and into his bedroom. He turned on the lights but kept them down low. They giggled as they fumbled trying to remove one another's clothing. He tripped as he moved back towards the bed. He fell back onto the bed and slid down to the floor and she toppled onto him. The alcohol was definitely having an impact.

It really wasn't the mad passionate scene they had each seen in the movies. But on the other hand, it did fit their relationship. The laughter took away the awkwardness and made it easy for them to be with one another. The first time they were playful with one another but once they recovered, the second time became a hot passionate intense scene.

She came close to saying she loved him a couple of times but caught herself. How could she possibly love him? They didn't know each other well enough. She didn't want to scare him away and yet it felt like they had been together forever. '*Wow, this day sure ended differently, then how it began,*' she thought to herself.

After the second time, they both lay satiated, drinking in what they had shared. He reached over and took her hand. He didn't want her to talk and he didn't want to cuddle, he just wanted to hold her hand and 'be' with her.

'*Oh good.*' she thought to herself, '*he knows how to just be.*' As they lay there, they moved into an 'out of body experience.' Both of them rose to the ceiling. They looked down on their bodies and then realized the other was 'out of body' as well. With that, they both crashed back into their bodies. Each turned to the other with a stumped look on their face. Neither of them had ever had an experience like that before.

"WOW!"

"Holy shit!"

"No kidding! Have you ever done that before?" he asked.

"No, have you?"

"No. How did that happen? You're the doctor. What just took place?" he pushed for answers.

"I have no idea and don't know if I want to know. Nobody ever taught anything about that in med school."

"I'm not sure I want to do that again. If we hold each other, maybe it will keep us grounded or something. That was weird. I think we must have had too much alcohol."

That sounded like a good excuse for her, too much alcohol. It was all an illusion. She rolled into his arms and hoped they could just go to sleep. She would wake up in the morning with a logical explanation.

Chapter 14

Infatuation, or...

They did fall asleep quickly; perhaps it was the wine; perhaps it was all the excitement of the day; perhaps it was to avoid thinking about what had happened; or more probably, it was a combination of everything.

Jasmine woke up first in the morning. Jordan was sound asleep. So, she went and had a shower, used his toothpaste and her finger to clean her teeth, then couldn't resist crawling back into bed with him.

She ran a hand over his chest and drew a finger up to his face. She outlined his mouth with her finger, thinking he was still asleep and wondering how she was going to wake him, then suddenly he grabbed her finger with his teeth scaring the living beejeezers out of her.

"How long have you been awake?' she got out between gasps.

"Ever since you crawled back into bed with me and I felt that wonderfully naked body next to mine," he opened his eyes and smiled. "I wanted to know what you were going to do to wake me up. I like waking up to you and I love what you are wearing," he couldn't believe what a love-sick teenager he sounded like again. "What time is it?"

As she rolled over to look at the clock on his night table, one of her girls slid outside the sheets. He didn't waste the opportunity. She loved it and she giggled as she slid back between the sheets. His hands and his mouth couldn't get enough of her. She loved the feel of his hands on her body, exploring, massaging, grabbing and she responded in kind. She loved that they could laugh and giggle and tease each other and their bodies. This time their love making had a very different feel as they made love in the full brightness of the morning sun. It didn't take long for their playfulness to morph into an intensity neither of them had ever shared with anyone else.

When they finished, neither of them wanted to look to the ceiling. They needed to stay grounded today. He didn't want to let go of her body, but they had to go to work. Wrapping an arm around her, he pushed her out of the bed with his body. "Shower time if we want to get actually get to work this morning," he explained as he pushed.

She wanted to see what it was like being in the shower with him though she had already had hers earlier. '*Oh well, who cares,*' she thought to herself and followed him into the shower. She decided she loved not only making love with him but showering with him. There was that 'love' word again, she had to be careful. She got out of the shower and got dressed. Now she needed to be quick or she was going to be late. She wanted to arrive, right on time even though being on time meant missing breakfast. She wanted to avoid reasons for questions and teasing from the rest of the staff.

She was already dressing by the time he came out of the shower and into the bedroom with the bath sheet wrapped around his midsection. Yup, he was a sexy man, no doubt about it. *'Focus here Jasmine,'* she told herself, *'You have to get work, on time!'* she clarified to herself.

He looked at the clock and looked at her, "I know I took you away yesterday and you need to be there on time today, but when are you finished your shift today? I will come by and pick you up. Actually, I need to get dressed quickly too and get you to work, you don't have a car," he thankfully realized because she hadn't given it a thought. He got dressed quickly as he promised. She went to find his car keys; found her purse and was at the front door only moments before him.

On the drive to work, he again asked her what her schedule was like for the day. She told him that barring any emergencies she should be finished by 5:30. He suggested he come and pick her up at her office. She agreed and suggested tonight they stay at her place for dinner. She was careful not to suggest he stay over at her place; dinner was sufficient.

However, he wasn't happy with just that, "Okay then tonight I will stay at your place and then we can bless your home as well. Let's go out for dinner. I will take you to my favorite restaurant and then we can go back and bless your place."

Once again, she was grinning from ear to ear, *'I had better get that grin off my face before I walk in,'* she admonished herself. But to Jordan she said, "Sounds great. I will look forward to it all day. I think I like blessings." She reached over for a kiss before getting out of the car. *'Now take that grin off your face,'* she scolded herself. But her body wasn't cooperating.

As she walked into the hospital, it seemed as if the whole ward was at the Admin desk with hands on their hips; grins on their faces; and raised eyebrows. They all wanted to know what Dr. Jasmine was up to. She hadn't dated since she had come to the hospital. And now she had a beau who not only was very good looking but who also showed up before work with flowers and balloons?

The grin obviously wasn't going to go away. So, she nodded at everyone and allowed her face to grin from ear to ear. As she walked by them, she looked each one in the eye. She didn't say a word. Really, didn't the grin say it all? A couple of the nurses refused to let her get away with that and ran after her.

"No way are we going to let you get away with that."

"What is his name?"

"How long have you known him?"

"Where did you meet?"

They had a load of questions. But she simply unlocked her office door, turned around to give them her biggest smile, then walked in and closed the door behind her.

It was a long day, not because it was a difficult day; or a tiring day; or an emotional day; but rather because she had to do everything she could think of to avoid questions. She wasn't ready to share anything yet. This was hers and she wanted to keep it to herself for a while longer. She needed to figure it out. Was this just infatuation, or was it the real thing?

If that weren't bad enough, she also had a difficult time staying focused on her work.

Chapter 15

Cloud 9

On the other side of town, Jordan walked in on 'cloud nine'. He loved his work; loved his research into 'Green' designs; loved the preparations he was engaged in to open up his own office though it was still a while away; and now he loved his private life too.

Jordan had really enjoyed his time with Jasmine in Africa. He had come home with all kinds of ideas and plans on how to make her coming home a real celebration. He had never felt like that with anyone else before. Was it love; was this the real thing; or was it all an illusion simply because they had been in a faraway place together?

He couldn't wait for her to come back. He almost ached to see her. Would it last over here, or would it just fizzle out because there was really no substance behind it?

He put everything on hold, when he got the call from his mother that they were in the hospital and his father had had a heart attack. Mom had reassured him Dad was okay, but he couldn't not go up, he just couldn't.

He came back as soon as he was sure his father was okay. He never told his family about Jasmine. On the one hand, they always minimized everything in his life anyway; on the other hand, he didn't know what her response would be like here, back in her home territory. But after the day they had yesterday, he wanted to tell the world. It was like they had simply taken up where they left off in Africa. In fact, their conversations yesterday covered a huge spectrum from the simple and shallow; to the deep and heavy; and they just kept going.

Then, last night! There wasn't any need to get comfortable with one another in bed or figure out what turned each other on, it was like they were simply meant for one another. He had never believed there was only one woman for each man out there and now he questioned his belief. It really did feel as if they were really meant for one another. Surely, this wasn't just an infatuation. If it was, it sure felt good.

Was this an infatuation? Would it last? Could they make the transition from Africa to Boston? Too many questions to answer; too much to think about when he had work to do. *'Come on Jordan, enough! Focus!'* he scolded himself.

He did go to work and he did focus, but his mind kept drifting off throughout the day. What would tonight be like? How could he make it special for her? He wanted to make all of life special for her. *'But you also have to work, now focus!'* he told himself for the umpteenth time that day.

He couldn't remember one date that had him struggling to focus the next day or anticipating the next night. He couldn't remember ever thinking of anyone in terms of a lifetime. *"God, man you got it bad,"* he decided by mid-afternoon.

He had always been the cool one; no one ever really attracted him. There were a lot of gals who chased him down and he knew he had been considered a 'real catch' in university. But this was the first time he had ever fallen for someone. There was an aspect to it he didn't like. He couldn't seem to get control of his thoughts. On the other hand, everything in life seemed more vibrant and alive and he did like that.

Two colleagues had already stopped in to ask if he was okay. One had figured it out and knew there was a woman involved but Jordan wasn't sharing anything yet, not until he felt in control of his thoughts and the situation.

He took time at lunch to phone a florist and ask for a big bouquet of orchids to send to Jasmine's office; then he phoned to make reservations at his favorite Greek restaurant. Again, things he had never done before. The only person he had ever sent flowers to, was his mom on her 75th birthday, and here, in just two days, he had two bought bouquets for Jasmine. He hadn't even asked her if she liked Greek. *"She had better"* he thought to himself, because it was one of his favorites.

When he was working on a project, like his current one, he often didn't leave the office till 8 or 9 at night. Tonight, he left right on time at 5 PM. He went straight to the hospital and walked in past the Admin Desk. This time a nurse stopped him asking him for his name. He explained he wasn't a patient, just here to pick up a doctor. One of the nurses, who had patiently waited out his explanation, said laughing, "Yes dear sir, we are more than aware you are not a patient. And we know which doctor you are here to pick up. We were, however, just wondering what your name was," she explained with a twinkle.

He didn't want to make matters worse for Jasmine and thought it was best she tell them what she wanted them to know; how much she wanted them to know; and when she wanted them to know it. So rather than answering their question, he responded with, "Well if you know the doctor I am here to pick up, then I would suggest you ask the doctor in question, whatever it is you would like to know."

He laughed when he heard the audible tones of frustration as he walked by the nurses refusing to answer their questions, *'Good answer, Jordan,'* he thought to himself as he walked down the hallway.

Jasmine wasn't in her office when he arrived, but the door was unlocked so he went in and sat down, hoping it would be a nice surprise for her to see him there when she returned. It was. She walked in looking deep in thought, but literally lit up when she saw him sitting waiting for her. Her expression made his whole day. She stood at the door and just beamed, then quickly moved into her office and closed the door behind her. "I am so glad to see you," was all she said.

He stood up and moved towards her to hold on for dear life, or was it a lifetime, he really wasn't sure. They just stood there and hugged. They didn't even kiss. They held on to each other as if their very lives depended on it. Eventually they moved back just enough to look deep into one another's eyes, or was it the souls; each asking if this was real?

"I think I am very infatuated with you Mr. Jordan," she offered him. "I wonder how long this will last?"

"You are the doctor, but I do believe you have made an incorrect diagnosis," he countered.

"Really, how is that, may I ask?"

"I have a strong sneaky suspicion we might actually be in love," he explained and bent down and took her mouth with a deep longing. Everything he gave, she returned in kind. As they kissed, her arms wrapped around him and her fingers moved through his hair and down along his face. His arms wrapped around her back, pulling her so close she seemed to move inside his very beingness, almost as if they were encased as one.

"How do we know this for sure?" she asked when they finally came up for air, "how do we know this isn't just an infatuation?"

"I am ready to spend a lifetime proving it to you."

"That sounds like something pretty serious," she looked at him with a puzzled expression. *Was he really proposing this soon? Really?'*

"I am willing to bet on it. Let's look at it this way. We experienced the hell of Africa together; came home six weeks apart; and finally got around to blessing our relationship. I can't get you out of my head and quite frankly don't want to. I have never experienced anything like this before and feel like a silly love-sick teenager. As we are supposed to be adult about these things? This is what I propose: we give ourselves time to confirm this is not some silly infatuation; then when the time is right, I create a romantic situation where I give you the kind of proposal you deserve; after a respectful, very short period of time, we have one of those big parties beginning with a "W." To top it off, we live happily ever after. How does this sound to you?"

She looked at him as if he was 'half out of his tree'. "I really don't know what to say Mr. Jordan, other than it sounds like a damn good plan." They sealed the deal with a kiss, and then went back to simply gazing into one another's eyes with wonder and amazement. Was it really this easy? Could this form the basis of a good healthy long-term relationship? Could their love last across time? There were so many questions they each had. But for right now, they just held one another. The rest would come in due time.

Chapter 16

Jasmini Loves Her Plants

It was a very hot time of year. Jasmini went to get her big bamboo hat to protect her head and body from the blistering sun. She needed to get water from the Ganges River. She attempted to cover her 'Ayurveda gardens' with sheets of cotton, to protect them from the sun. When it got this hot in Allahabad, the plants needed more water.

Her father and her husband, Janardan, were renowned Ayurveda healers. She attended to the gardens growing the special plants they used in all their formulations. She had numerous gardens: some exposed to the sun; some hidden beneath a huge castor plant with massive leaves for those needing to grow in the shade; one garden was above the ground with a built-in drainage system, so the soils were dry for the plants that thrived in desert like conditions; and another was near the waterway for those plants requiring damp wet soils.

She knew her plants like the back of her hand, which ones liked one another, and which ones needed to be grown a part. She was known for her green thumb. Anything and everything she grew thrived.

In addition to growing the plants, she also knew the particulars about harvesting them: which ones had more nutrients when harvested before the rising of the sun; which liked to be harvested in the hot sun; and which preferred to be harvested in the coolness of the evenings.

After the growing and the harvesting came the processing. Some liked to be dried out flat; other preferred to be hung; and others liked to be rolled.

Jasmini's mother and grandmother had taught her since she was a small child how to get the most from their gardens. Her father and husband's plants needed to be in the best condition to provide the most medicinal capacity for the formulations.

All in all, Jasmini grew over 500 different plants which she harvested and provided for the formulations. Many belonged to the same genus but had several different species and she knew them all. Although her role was to grow the foods and herbs and spices, she also knew much of the formulating. She had watched and questioned her father about his formulas since she was very young: what went with what; how and why different plants were combined; and what were used for what types of ailments?

She particularly enjoyed working with the sugar disorders. There were 20 sugar disorders each requiring a different formulation. She knew her husband took great pride in his work as he was able to swiftly identify which sugar pattern afflicted the person. But for her, she was more interested in the particular formulation that needed to be given for the diagnosis. As soon as a client came in and her husband identified the sugar pattern, Jasmini was off and running; pulling, cutting, and crushing the necessary herbs to make the formulation she knew her husband would prescribe.

Chapter 17

Choosing the Right Husband

She loved her work and was so glad when her parents chose her husband for her. She was concerned they might choose a husband working in a different profession than her father, but she hadn't needed to worry. They understood her passion. As a Brahmin, she was groomed and trained to work in the healing capacity. They wanted a special husband to complement her gifts of understanding plant life and took their time interviewing possible husbands for her.

They were wealthy and came from a well-recognized Brahmin family. In addition, Jasmini was a beautiful young woman. She walked with the grace of a princess but had a humble air about her. She was a vulnerable young woman that needed someone who would take good care of her; someone who would love and treasure her as much as her family did. While they took their time to find the gentleman who would fill their criterion, Jasmini worked patiently in her gardens. She questioned, once in a while, whether she would ever get married, then would push the doubt away and focus on her plants.

Eventually her parents found the man to love and cherish her. He too was a Brahmin and an Ayurvedic physician like her father. He had grown up with the highest of the Ayurvedic morals, and honor and integrity. He was a kind and good-hearted man with a great sense of humor. Jasmini was very glad when her parents finally introduced her to Janardan.

The courtship lasted a prolonged time. The parents needed to get to know one another. Then Janardan and Jasmini were allowed small amounts of supervised time together. They walked through all the required formal steps until the month came when they were to be married.

As with all Brahmin weddings of the time, their wedding was a prolonged affair lasting a full moon's cycle. There were the celebrations for the groom; celebrations for the bride; and celebrations between the family; and finally, the wedding day.

It was a beautiful wedding, full of color and light and gold, with over a 1000 people. Entertainers performed wedding dances and fertility dances and the food went on forever. And finally, it was time for the bride and groom to leave so they could bless one another.

Jasmini was very shy. Her mother had told her all about the wedding night and what it would entail. She knew her father had spoken with Janardan about how to take care of his daughter. But she was still apprehensive. Janardan was also anxious, he did not want to disappoint his new wife. They talked well into the night and decided they would wait a day. He didn't really want to wait, but he was concerned about how apprehensive Jasmini was. He had heard about how some wives got scared on their wedding night and then never wanted to give again. He didn't want that and was prepared to do whatever was needed to ensure Jasmini enjoyed their shared time.

The moment Janardan suggested they wait until Jasmini was less anxious, she gave him her heart. That he was willing to respect her and wait for her was the most precious gift he could have given her. When she woke in the morning, she shyly told him it was time to share her sacredness with him. He loved that she willingly gave of herself and was very careful with her. He knew the first time might hurt her and was careful not to let that happen. It was a very gentle experience and one creating the way for a love to develop between them that would cross over time.

Their love deepened very quickly. It began with a respect and reverence for one another and deepened into a passionate longing.

They both had a love of spirituality providing them with long deep discussions. They had both trained in-depth and understood how consciousness crossed many levels of awareness. Their beliefs required that men and women meditated every day although in separate places. They followed the beliefs they were brought up with but also learned to meditate together in the privacy of their home. With spiritual guidance, they also learned how they could go beyond the limitations of their bodies and unite on another plane, another energetic level of experience.

They became very adept at their skill. The point where they met was beyond time and place; their souls mingling and communicating in a way their bodies could not. It was a magnificent way to deepen the love between them.

Eventually over time, it allowed them to connect and communicate when their bodies were apart. If Janardan needed help with a client or for a given formulation, he would reach out and connect with Jasmini, in another dimension, and she would prepare it for him. If she needed help at home, she could connect with him and let him know he needed to come home. They were very careful not to abuse their ability, in case the gods took it away from them.

They came from a place of gratitude and appreciation, in life in general, and with their gift.

Chapter 18

Building a home

Eventually Jordian and Juliana made their way to the community where Merlin had directed Jordian. It was a small community, surrounded by beautiful forests with lush fertile lands within it.

Jordian rode to a place outside of the community where he wanted to build the barraca they had discussed. As they travelled to the community, he watched the angles of the sun and the moon. Now he knew exactly where the best place would be for a barraca. One that could accommodate the designs they had decided upon. They worked together identifying the needs required by her seeds and decided upon one regular garden and five different 'special gardens'. His design would also enable her to work with her gems and crystals, in special waters dancing as if in a waterfall.

They had created the design and now they had the location. They went into the community to see if there was any issue that would prevent them from starting to build their creation. The people were open and welcoming and loved that Juliana was a healer. When Jordian offered to help them design irrigation paths for their farms, everyone was delighted.

Within a moon, the basics of the barraca were completed and they moved into their abode. During the designing, building and planting, they were very respectful of one another though the tension between them was building. They touched one another often in passing but never let it go any further.

Tonight, was going to be the celebration of their union. Juliana had exchanged some of the funds Merlin had left her for materials to make a few candles and buy a few special foods to celebrate their first night together.

Jordian had exchanged some of what he had for hay to lay their blankets on, so Juliana would have comfort. He knew it would be her first time. He had some experience behind him and he hoped he would be able to make it easier for her.

The full moon made a path through the open doors and the bare windows as if to provide its own blessing. The night was warm with a gentle scented breeze. Juliana loved all the scents around this community. Many good herbs and spices grew here and tonight the lavender flooded their senses as the breeze danced in the candlelight. It was a good gentle loving experience for both of them. Jordian explained to Juliana he knew they could make love in a number of different ways with different emotions, however tonight he would be gentle and careful with her. And he was. And it was good.

Juliana was delighted with the pleasure and asked Jordian for more and he gave, and eventually they slept in each other's arms. In the morning, they shared each other's body again. They were like children this time, playing and laughing with delight.

The men from the community came every morning to help Jordian work on his Barraca. This morning, their arrival brought their love making to a quick halt. They knew they would have that night and every night for the rest of their lives to love and share, so they quickly got up and prepared to work on their barraca.

Chapter 19

Children

Juliana came out of her reverie as Jordian walked through the door. She turned to hug him and welcome him home. He saw she had been crying and wanted to know what was wrong. She explained she was simply reflecting on old experiences. She shared she had moved from thinking of her 'Merlin' when he crossed over to how they met and how they came to build their barraca.

Jordian smiled. He knew she often did that. The tears were good. She shared with Jordian so much of her experiences with 'Merlin' that Jordian felt he knew the old Master himself.

In a similar vein, Jordian shared much of his travels and his experiences with Juliana. She loved to hear of the far-off places he had traveled and the people he had met. She also shared his love of how differently homes were designed and the special attributes a given community may have developed.

She let go of Jordian and went to attend her small child before beginning the preparations for dinner.

It was their third. She knew it would be her last and she was okay with that. She had enough to do with all of her clients;

her garden; her children; and of course, the special times spent with Jordian.

She loved her children. The whole experience of knowing when the seed had connected; to feeling the development occurring in her womb; even the child birthing was a fascinating experience. And once those beautiful little innocents began growing and exploring the world around them, they were always such a delight. She paid special attention to her diet before, during and after a pregnancy so her body provided the best home for growth and development for her children. She talked with each and stroked her belly as they developed; never stopping the touching and stroking and telling them how much she loved them when they emerged from her sacredness.

As Merlin had told her it would be, so it was. They were strong good children and she loved them dearly, almost as much as she loved her Jordian.

Chapter 20

Energies with Ayurveda

Jasmini and Janardan worked with an evolved master called Babaji. Both opportunities and responsibilities came with being born into Brahmi families. The two were provided with training and direction to develop their inner beings, or true selves. Both Janardan and Jasmini loved this kind of work. They spent much time together engaged in various spiritual practices, with Babaji, to enhance their capacities.

Babaji taught them to communicate telepathically from wherever they were; he taught them how to see the energetics of living things. This was a beautiful gift for Janardan; it allowed him to identify body imbalances. Initially, it was all about the external energetics but as he developed his gift, he learned to see the energetic pathways of the marma meridians running through the body and supporting all. In Traditional Chinese Medicine, marma meridians came to be known as acupuncture meridians; but it took a long time before allopathic medicine recognized the meridians and the energy that flowed through them.

When a patient came through the door, Janardan identified the person's dosha. An Ayurveda understanding of the combination between: the energetic field; physiological metabolism; cognitive and emotional style; and personality. Janardan would then identify what stage of imbalance the dosha was in merely by looking at the person. He simply asked the person to stand in the room and slowly turn around. He would observe the energetic patterns running through and around the person. These patterns revealed what the body required to re-establish balance and harmony again.

Most practitioners used long extensive intakes of over a 1000 questions to determine the predominant energy pattern in the person, but with training in the energetic fields, Janardan learned to identify the patterns simply by looking at the body. Simply by looking at the body's energetics, he could determine the body's dosha; stage of dysfunction; and the protocol required for healing.

Even his father-in-law was very impressed with his capacities.

Once the dosha was established, then a practitioner would determine what was wrong with the dosha. An imbalanced dosha could evolve through six stages to cause imbalance and symptoms in the body:

Accumulation: too much dosha (Vata, Pitta, Kapha) energy in one area

Aggravation: the energy/dosha creates a qualitative change in the dosha and moves beyond its normal place causing a 'vitiation' or abnormality

Dissemination: now the energy/dosha moves out of its home place and starts to circulate through the body creating low-grade, non-specific symptoms, i.e., fatigue, depression, achiness, just not feeling well.

Localization: now the dosha localizes in a tissue outside its normal place and begins to disrupt the functioning of another tissue or organ. Several factors determine where this location might be: abnormality in channels, i.e., blood vessels or lymph channels; or digestive toxins called ama. Ayurveda medicine identified many different types of ama throughout the body and recognized how they affect the body differently. But the digestive amas, were usually involved with imbalances in the body.

Manifestation: now the dosha can be identified as a developing disease; tissues are disrupted.

Disruption: the abnormal dosha is now embedded in the tissue and the body's natural repair processes are unable to reverse it; it is likely to become chronic. Again, using a Kapha example, it might become a chronic or perennial sinusitis or rhinitis

Once the dosha/energy imbalance was identified; and the stage it had progressed to identified; then the practitioner outlined the particular healing protocol that person required for healing. Sometimes the body required various forms of cleansing and detoxing known panchakarma.

First, they would saturate the body with herbal and medicated oils (a Snehan) to provide the body with nutrients to strengthen the body. Often it included a Snehan, where herbs and steam are utilized, similar to a modern day sauna, to provoke the body to loosen and excrete toxins.

Next, in accordance with: what was out of balance; what dosha the person was; and the stage of imbalance; a detoxification treatment was provided. The four most commonly used detoxifications methods were:

Vamana: a forced vomiting used for upper respiratory issues like asthma and eliminating toxins from the upper gut

Virechan: a purging used for the lower gut and bowel issues including arthritis, asthma cough, boils, cataracts, chronic fever, constipation, diabetes, facial discoloration, intestinal disorders, jaundice, piles, skin diseases, spleen enlargement, tumors, womb issues, and ailments in the head like depression

Vasti: a medicinal enema and the most common treatment. The classical Ayurveda Text 'Ashtanga Hridaya' says, "A purge properly carried out leads to clarity of intellect, power to the organs, elemental stability and glow to digestive fire and it delays aging"

Nasya: includes three types of nasal administration usually applied to anything above the neck. It is typically used for issues like facial paralysis and it is known to stop graying

The protocols ranged from the very simplistic to the very complex. Once the person eliminated the toxins causing the problem, Janardan worked at strengthening and rebuilding the body's capacity to perform optimally again.

Sometimes the protocols involved the psyche and how the person thought. Other times, it was the body that impacted on the mind and how the mind functioned. They recognized not only that the mind and body were much interwoven; but, in particular, how interwoven the mind was with processes of the gut.

Janardan developed very well under Babaji and cultivated a worthy reputation as an Ayurveda physician. When he wasn't working helping people get well, he loved to design, create and build special gardens for his beloved Jasmini. Her love and ability to entice plants to grow and thrive was amazing and he always wanted to make things easier for her.

As they experimented, they learned unusual things about plants. They of course, already knew some plants thrived in the hot dry sun; whereas others loved damp wet feet; some liked to be surrounded by others while some preferred to be alone. Plants were a lot like people, each thriving in a different environment. Experimentation, however, revealed many more interesting things about plants. Some love to hear the water splashing down the waterways he made for her, whereas others preferred the quiet; some enjoyed the vibrations provided by different gems and crystals, while others didn't. There were so many things one could play with to help plants thrive, just like with people.

Jasmini also learned how to move beyond the physical senses. With in-depth training, from Babaji, the two were able to move out of the five dimensions and into other worlds. Babaji explained that when they worked together as they did, it enhanced both their love and their capacity.

He taught them how to go both forward and backward in time, which, once one moved past the five limiting dimensions of the earth plane, was relatively simple. He taught them to use their gift wisely and with discipline, otherwise they would lose their gift and spend several lifetimes recovering what they had lost.

He continued to teach them various other kinds of lessons and enhance their capacities. He had already taught Janardan to see the people energetics. Now he worked with Jasmini to help her see the plant energies. Plants were alive beings with immune systems and respiratory systems and all kinds of systems similar to human beings. Just touching a plant provoked a complexity of enzyme reactivity. Plants also had the ability to communicate with each other and let each other know when pathogenic enemies were around

As Jasmini developed the ability to see the plant energies, she learned even more. The experimentation she previously engaged in was now considered very childlike. She was now able to go way beyond that simple form of defining, measuring and observing. It was like the plants talked with her on a whole different level. Their energies expanded and flowed when they were happy; shrink and contract when they were afraid. If the plants didn't work together, their energies would knot up; If something caused overstimulation, static rays would jump out from them. It was amazing how similar their energies were to human energies; their energies reacted and responded, though in different environments, comparably to human emotional responses.

Jasmini grew 100s of herbs, but her favorite herbs, which complimented Janardan's healings, included:

Ashwagandha

A beautiful herb provoking general healing in the body, which later became known as the *'Indian ginseng'*. As an adaptogenic herb Ashwagandha supports the adrenals. It is also a mild sedative and muscle relaxant for the central nervous system. It increases the white blood cells in the immune system. It helps to support the endocrine or hormonal system. It regulates cholesterol thus supporting the cardiac system. And it supports the reproductive system by increasing libido.

Bacopa

Typically used for the mind. It has bacosides that have a positive influence on brain cells and the regeneration of brain tissue; it protects infants from neonatal hypoglycemia; benefits the liver by encouraging a liver detox and boosting effective liver function; combats stress as an adaptogenic herb. Finally, bacosides helps enhance the benefits of pain killers, like morphine, while reducing the addictive high and protecting organs from opiate toxicity.

Elethrocococcus

Later became known as Siberian ginseng, another adaptogenic used to stimulate resistance to stress and restore vitality; support the Immune System; regulate blood sugars and cholesterols; improve memory and help to regulate some hormones.

Ginger

A powerful anti-inflammatory and anti-viral used for arthritis, bronchitis, coughs, fevers, headaches and nausea. Ginger is also used to improve appetite, eliminate dyspepsia symptoms, regulate cholesterol and blood pressure and prevents internal blood clots

Glycyrrhiza: (aka licorice root)

Contains many anti-depressant compounds and most commonly used for adrenal fatigue and healing ulcers; is excellent for a number of gut issues including inflammatory and spasm symptoms; and boosts interferons in the immune system making it anti-viral.

Gynnostemma pentophyllum

Another adaptogenic herb, with over 80 known saponins, helps to protect the body and recover from both physical and mental stresses; increases white blood cells to support the immune system; cleanses the stomach and the intestines to support the digestive system; regulates cholesterol, triglycerides and blood pressure to support the cardio system.

Sandalwood

Have anti-septic, anti-inflammatory, anti-spasmodic, carminative, diuretic, hypotensive, muscle relaxant (both skeletal and smooth muscles) and sedative properties. There are several different varieties with the Indian species being the best; the older the tree, the better the essential oil from the bark.

Triphala

A famous Ayurveda formulation of three herbs: amalaki, bibhitaki and haritaki with huge benefit for all aspects of the gastrointestinal tract. Triphala benefits the entire body by balancing the dosha energies (Vata, Pitta, and Kapha).

Turmeric

Contains curcumin, a well-recognized anti-inflammatory, anti-oxidant, anti-cancer, anti-tumor, and an anti-depressant; it boosts the brain's neurotrophic factor, strengthens the lining of blood vessels; curcumin crosses the blood brain barrier and clears out amyloid plaque that can cause Alzheimer's.

As Jasmini's and Janardan's capacity to move past time and space increased; they also learned to move into other realms of more and more subtle energies; now both were able to learn from others and teach others on the subtler energies.

Chapter 21

Questions

Jordan's and Jasmine's relationship developed and flourished over the time period Jordan had planned out for them.

They found they enjoyed one another's humor and laughter. They enjoyed philosophical discussions which could take them far into the night.

They both had a passion for their work. They decided he would open his private office after they got married. She was so excited for him. One day she might go into private practice as well, but for now the hospital paid well and she worked with a wide variety of patients.

In the meantime, she brought in a good salary and it would tide them over till he got his company well established. He was very concerned he might become dependent on her for periods of time if his company didn't flourish and he couldn't market what he wanted. His work was very specialized, although he was hoping it would take off over time, but it would probably take a while.

He had no problem dealing with these issues, when it was only him. He could live on virtually nothing for a period, but he did not want to drain Juliana, and he didn't want it to be a stressor for her, or to their relationship.

They talked a lot about it over the next few months. They went into elaborate detail with the worst-case scenarios including determining when 'enough was enough' and he would go back and work for another company. Or would he be able to continue his work on the side while working for someone else?

What if the shoe were on the other foot? How would they work it then? What if it required long hours that left Jasmine alone? Would he have an office at home and could he work for long hours from there? What would she be doing while he worked?

She wanted to learn about other forms of medicine. Western medicine tended to manage symptoms more than resolve issues and she wanted to resolve issues. She wanted to learn the nutrients the body required to heal. She wanted to learn the herbs so powerfully used around the world and the basis of many Western prescriptions. She wanted to use the REAL thing, not a synthetic man-made substitute. Did she need a separate office, or would they share an office? How much room did they require to do the work they wanted to do?

They also addressed where they would live. His apartment was better suited to both and already had an office he could work from. If they reorganized his office, she could have a bookshelf and desk to accommodate her research.

Her apartment was so austere, there was little for her to bring; they could incorporate most of it.

Did they want children? When and where? Or conversely, did they want to travel and work with projects around the world? If they did that, would she be able to do it with a private practice or would she be better off at a hospital?

Would they be able to apply for projects as a team; projects needing buildings constructed AND a physician. They started to investigate various programs and projects around the world. It was when they started their research that he began to really appreciate her capacity as a physician. She loved medicine and loved being able to help people, however she wanted to resolve the issues not merely manage the symptoms. She believed the REAL medicine other cultures utilized may actually have better remedies than the synthetics she was taught to use, and she wanted to know what they were and how to use them. She wanted to read the research behind them.

She had always had an issue with Conventional medicine just prescribing synthetic drugs. Why were they not learning about the nutrients the body required? Wouldn't it make more sense to learn about the vitamins and minerals; the different omega 3 fatty acids and amino acids; all the different phytonutrients the body required to do what it needed to do?

When they took one course on CAM (Complementary and Alternative Medicine) her biggest question was why, as medical doctors, they were not studying more of this? Unfortunately, the course simply provided a definition and an overview of the different healing modalities. There was a strong overtone that the alternative healing modalities didn't really have any evidence. However, when Jasmine researched them, there was a ton of information in well-designed clinical studies. The studies just weren't in the typical medical journals that, she quickly learned, were controlled Big Pharma.

One night she really got going with Jordian. "I don't get it?" she explained. "The body produces over a million red blood cells a minute. It also has to produce over 10,000 enzymes; over a hundred neurotransmitters and neuropeptides; over 50 different types of hormones; and the list goes on and on when it comes to what it creates for the Immune System. It obviously needs nutrients to do all that. Why are we not learning about this? When you really get into researching most of the pharmaceuticals, they are really designed to manage symptoms! AND, if that weren't bad enough, investigative research shows that these prescriptions really don't achieve what they are supposed to or are claimed to! We are supposed to be helping people get better. That's what I went to med school for! Not to pump people full of synthetic drugs that simply manage symptoms. AND, do you know, most of these synthetic drugs actually deplete the body of nutrients?

Now what's that all about? When you read the fine print, so many of the drugs actually cause diabetes, stroke, heart attacks, cancer, and on and on. It doesn't make sense. Why are we not going to the route of the problem? Why are we just managing the symptoms?" She had so many questions.

They made a point of balancing the time they spent together. Whether they were researching 'Green' designs for Jordan or whether they were researching nutrition and herbal medicine and how these helped the body actually engage in healing, for Jasmine.

He loved the fact she went beyond the confines of what she was taught in med school. And she loved the fact he went beyond the confines of what he was taught in architectural school. They often turned to one another laughing at what a great pair they made.

Chapter 22

Children and Herbs

Although Jordian's seed did not produce immediately, they did not worry about having children. They both believed and accepted Merlin's prediction that Juliana would have three. So, they simply agreed to enjoy their time together and when it was meant to be, it would be.

Their home was finished, and Juliana's gardens flourished. She often sat in her garden reflecting on all Merlin had taught her. He had taught her about many 'foolishness's' people associated with plants. Then he made sure what she remembered were the healing components of each. Juliana's favorite herbs included.

Aconite or monkshood

This deadly perennial native plant, needed to grow in a shady place, had a tall stem of about five feet and produced a beautiful purple flower in the early summer. Although a dangerous plant if not used properly, it could be used for fevers, inflammation, lung infections and nerve tingling.

Ambrette seed

Merlin told her he collected it from a far-off land named India. He taught her to use it to stimulate the body or resolve gut cramps. He told her some peoples used it treat headaches, and when it was mixed with milk, it could treat itching and other skin conditions.

Anemones

This was another special plant from a far off place. Merlin taught her there were many legends about how the plant evolved that he thought were quite funny. More importantly, the plant was used to cure gout, leprosy and the common cold.

Angelica

Merlin taught her that there were many types of Angelica and it was used for different things around the world. The seeds he had for her, were to strengthen the heart and the immune system; and it was good for gut related issues and reproductive issues, as well as a diaphoretic.

Apple

It was a beautiful tree and he had many varieties. Merlin explained the apple tree grew tall and strong and needed a lot of room. There were many more types than the ones he was giving her. Hers provided a fruit that was tart and very crunchy. She was told not to use the soft sweet kinds for medicinal purposes. The apple tree only produced once a year and would provide shade for other plants through the year. It was known to help regulate stools, blood sugars and cholesterols; protect the brain from issues which, many lifetimes in the future, would come to be known as Parkinson's and Alzheimer's; plus, it could be fermented into a very useful cider that could be used for 101 different issues.

Arnica

Another ancient medicinal plant used by many different civilizations as a good herb to stimulate the peripheral blood system; for any kind of bruise or sprain, muscle aches; and for insect bites. However, it could be very toxic if swallowed, which made proper handling essential. This led them to spend a lot of time working with it.

Basil

Merlin explained there were many varieties of basil. Each land had its own species and use for different purposes. Growers used it to help ground the soil so other plants would thrive. It was associated with everything from love to hate which told Jasmine how wide its uses could be. The basil had a wide variety of nutrients and Merlin liked to add it to a variety of formulas; as an anti-inflammatory (in the joints; in the gut and in the upper respiratory system); for upper respiratory tract infections; and other issues.

Betony

Although it had an interesting history associated with Christ, Merlin wanted her to use it to cure many ills. He explained uses for issues associated with both the body (from jaundice to gout to wheezing) and the mind (from headaches to neuralgia to convulsions).

Blackberry

Merlin insisted the blackberry be planted far away from anything else. Not only did it have thorns, but it would take over anything and everything in its path. He explained some peoples used it to keep evil spirits away, but he thought that was silliness. He told her to use it to tighten the skin, improve the mind, and reduce inflammation.

Camphor Laurel

The plant was grown for its camphor, which he warned again, can be poisonous if used incorrectly. It could safely be used to stimulate the digestive system; for inflammation; and as an anti-microbial.

Cedar

Another large tree with a wondrous scent used both internally & externally for skin disorders; to strengthen the Immune System; for anti-inflammatory issues; as a diuretic; and to resolve a number of different issues.

Chicory

Merlin always started to laugh when talking about chicory, explaining some people thought it had the magical ability of making a person invisible. He wanted her to use chicory for liver and blood problems. It could also be used like dandelions.

Cinnamon

This was one of Merlin's favorites. It had been used by the Egyptian Pharaohs for embalming and for gifts. Medicinally, it was used for a number of different issues from sweet imbalances in the blood to women's moon cycles.

Cumin

Another plant making Merlin laugh was black cumin. Some peoples believed it would give you everlasting life because it was the 'cure all' for anything and everything.

Merlin claimed it did have a huge number of nutrients and so perhaps some of the claims were true. In addition, many problems originated in the gut and black cumin was great for the gut and digestive issues like diarrhea, colic, bowel cramps/spasms, bloating/gas and could be used for reproductive issues like starting a menstrual flow or as an aphrodisiac. It also worked for insomnia and to improve the immune system.

Daisy

There were many species of daisies and many false stories. Merlin taught Juliana the plant was used to treat everything from insanity to small pox internally; and everything from broken bones to skin rashes externally. However, she was to use it for its cleansing properties in the gut; the fiber would move the stool; and the bitters would improve the appetite.

Dill

Merlin taught Juliana many purposes for dill both culinary and medicinal. It was great when mixed with water for colicky babies; for adults, when they had indigestion; and for a variety of stomach conditions; it acts as an anti-bacterial, anti-oxidant, and promotes production of a compound that they would call glutathione, in the distant future.

Fennel

Fennel was another herb Merlin taught was great for the gut; from weight to kidney, to spleen, to liver, to a number of different imbalances in the gut; to psychological issues like depression and anxiety.

Foxglove

Merlin warned the about the abuse of this plant and had all kinds of stories about what people believed about the magic of foxglove and foxes. He claimed the truth about foxglove had to do with stimulating muscle tissues; blood vessels; the kidneys and the heart.

Frankincense

Merlin had a real affinity for the small tree producing tiny white and pink flowers, called Frankincense. The essential oil can used for everything from respiratory infections to rheumatoid arthritis and even syphilis and tumors; for inflammatory issues; immune issues; and to help relieve stress and anxiety.

Garlic

Merlin loved this herb and claimed it could be used for the heart, blood, liver, and immune system.

Heather

Heather was very good in incredibly small doses. It was more used for psychological issues than physiological.

Iris

This plant was best when mixed with Scottish mead and used to generally strengthen the Immune System, the liver and the gut (nausea, vomiting and colic).

Juniper

Merlin taught Juliana to take the berries make an alcohol, and then mix it with golden raisins as a good pain killer. On its own it could be used as a detox agent and as an antiseptic.

Lemon Balm

It was a particularly good herb to be used for the heart, and in particular, with the heart and emotional issues.

Meadowsweet

A good herb used to calm the gut and strengthen the mucosal lining of the gut and for respiratory problems and arthritis.

Peppermint

She was taught to use this herb for teas, as a balm for toothaches; internally for digestive issues especially like inflammatory gut issues and respiratory issues like sore throats, colds, coughs, asthma and allergies.

Roman & German Chamomile

Another one of Merlin's favorites, though her caution was to make sure she didn't mix her chamomiles. The Roman one could be used for all kinds of digestive issues, insomnia, muscle spasms, and skin conditions.

Rosemary

A great kitchen herb and also used for some 1001 things: with anti-bacterial, anti-oxidant, anti-inflammatory, anti-fungal, and anti-septic properties.

Saffron

An important herb for Buddhists monks, though Merlin wanted her to use as an anti-oxidant and immune modulators; and for cancer and infections.

Sandalwood

Another herb Merlin collected from far off India, the land beyond. There were three categories of Sandalwood with many different uses for the herb. Merlin wanted her to focus on its use for mental disorders to calm the agitated mind, and to open doors for those who were more spiritually inclined.

Stinging nettles

Helps the body to get rid of excess water; eliminate joint pain; treat the prostate; cleanse and strengthen the blood; regulates blood sugars; clears skin conditions; almost anything.

Yarrow

Merlin claimed yarrow was used around the world as one of the most expansive herbs covering a wide variety of ills. Internally, it acted as an anti-inflammatory; an anti-microbial; in the digestive and central nervous system. Externally, it could be used for sores and rashes and wounds.

Withania aka Ashwagandha

A great healing herb, belonging to the tomato family, though the taste belongs to something else entirely. It relieves stress, fatigue, lack of energy, and concentration; protects the Immune System; enhances the brain functions; regulates cholesterols & blood sugars; and enhances the sex drive.

Of all of her plants, Juliana loved Stinging Nettles, Yarrow and Ashwagandha the best. They just seemed to help resolve almost anything.

Jordian's and Juliana's life together was as it should be. In the extended community Jordian created and designed water ways for irrigation and different styles of homes to live in. Along the way, he developed an excellent reputation. People loved the designs he created for their home. They were a unique couple and drew a lot of attention. Consequently, when royal families wanted something, he was asked, or rather told, to come and create their requests. From these royal commissions, he was bestowed a knighthood and Juliana began calling him, My Lord. He in turn called her, My Lady.

This evolved into a ritual to let each other know it was a good time to share their bodies. He loved that she loved to share her body with him and enjoyed taking pleasure from him. It was something that lasted for a life time. They never did tire of one another and, like Merlin had promised, it was a love that continued to grow richer with time.

No matter how often he was away, or what his work entailed, he promised himself he would always make Juliana feel she was the most important person on the face of the earth; to him.

Juliana never made that kind promise to herself about Jordian. She never thought of it. She just simply lived it. He was her passion, her reason for being. Yes, she knew she had a gift of healing people; they travelled for many moons to come to her for healing. But above and beyond it all was her Jordian. He was first and foremost in her life. And she loved to refer to him as 'My Lord'.

He didn't like to leave Juliana and she didn't like to be without him, nor did she want to leave her gardens in case she lost any of her precious plants. So, they often commuted. He would create designs and leave it to others to build and so he could come back home to his wife; he would go to help when necessary. If the trips were during times her gardens could manage without her, she would accompany him, and otherwise, she might meet him somewhere in between. She was a good horsewoman and could cover ground as fast as any man.

When the children started to come, she could no longer leave their homestead. He hated to leave Juliana and the children. Over time, however, Merlin worked with them. He started with their dreams to help them connect with himself and then with each other. Eventually, he taught them how to connect with each other when awake and in different places.

By the time the children came, they had developed a good capacity to see and communicate with one another when apart. An added benefit for Juliana was she could connect with Merlin if she was having any challenge working with a formulation.

Chapter 23

Three Children

And now, something new was starting to happen. Merlin had told Juliana she would develop the capacity to 'cross over' after she gave birth to her third child. Every day she waited, in anticipation for some sign, some experience; some communication from Merlin, that the new phase of her life was beginning.

When they were preparing for Merlin to cross over, she was too consumed with the preparations and never thought to ask how it would start and he had never volunteered the information. Then one night, it happened. Jordian called her My Lady all through dinner so she knew they would be making love again tonight. She prepared a lovely candle with the scent of Jasmine. The jasmine grew in the special heated garden and produced the most beautiful essential oils. The candle danced in the moonlight as the moon made a path through their window and bathed their bodies in light. The gentle summer breeze gently moved the various scents from the garden and her candle, around the moonlit room. Unlike many homes, where everyone slept in the same room, Jordian made a separate room for the children. The separation, and the materials between the walls, allowed them a privacy most did not have.

They started playfully giggling like children, then their lovemaking evolved into an intensity moving both of them. When they were satiated, they fell back onto the bed gasping for air. Jordian reached over and took her hand in his. Then she was gone; out of her body and she was watching their bodies from above. Yet, she was still holding Jordian's hand. Jordian was there, with her, looking down from above. He had an astonished look on his face. Then they 'crashed' back into their bodies.

Jordian jumped up from the bed. "What the hell was that?" he asked her, the heavens, he wasn't sure who he was asking.

Juliana sat up with glee. She knew what was happening and was thrilled Jordian was experiencing it with her. She patted the bed beside her, for him to sit down. She told him of what Merlin had shared with her in the year before he crossed over. She knew something was going to start to happen after she had her third child.

"Why haven't you told me of this?" he demanded. That was a pretty strange experience and he had no forewarning.

"I have told you most everything Merlin told me. I really couldn't tell you about this as I really didn't know how or when it would happen, so I didn't know what to tell you. I can share with you what I remember him saying." she offered. She explained that Merlin had told she would develop a 'cross over,' capacity which apparently was common in different cultures throughout history. All she really knew was she would be able to go into 'different planes' and cross over time. It was a gift that would grow over time, although she didn't know how. She had no idea

Jordian would be a part of it. She had been anxiously waiting for it to start ever since their third child was born but had no idea what she was actually waiting for. She was thrilled it finally started and even more thrilled he was a part of it.

He listened carefully to all she shared. He had never heard of things of this nature before. But now that there was some sort of reference for it, he was willing to work with it. She eliminated the fear for him. And what could he say, if Merlin was involved, then it must be okay.

"So, what are we supposed to do now?" he wanted to know. She didn't know. She just knew she was excited about the process and she would be watching and ready for it. She assumed Merlin would come to one of them, to give them direction; they just needed to be patient.

Over time, the ability to be out of their bodies grew. They were able to move around with it; in and out of the house with it. Jordian hated to let Juliana know how scared he was. Rising above your body and looking down on it was one thing; they had done that often enough now; but moving out of the barraca? What if they couldn't get back? They had children to look after.

But Juliana had no fear. She trusted completely and with this came the ability. She learned to go in and out of their home and across the country side. She took Jordian with her, albeit somewhat reluctantly. They were now able to journey with purpose and intent. It was fun. They would make love and satiate one another and then they would travel.

Then one night, something happened, it was different. They looked at one another with question. What was up? Then they saw Merlin. Juliana got so excited she lost her focus and was back lying on their bed before she knew it.

"Damn," she said out loud and heard Merlin and Jordian laugh at her. She focused and allowed her body's energy to go again. "Oh Merlin, it is so good to see you again."

"Yes, but realize you are not seeing my physical body, any more than you or Jordian are in your physical bodies. I told you I would always be with you. Now you are beginning to understand. I have been watching as you and Jordian have learned to travel without your physical bodies. You have done well, My Child, although you are no longer a child. You have grown into a beautiful young woman with children of your own. And I watched as Jordian built you the beautiful gardens you attend to so well. Now we will be moving on with your next lesson," with that he was gone.

Jordian and Juliana looked at one another. Another lesson, but he was gone? What were they to learn?

They had no need to talk in this place; their voices communicated in a very different way. They simply knew each other's thoughts.

"You are not paying attention, My Child," they heard Merlin say. But where was he? Neither of them could see Merlin physically in this plane. "Use your inner eye," Merlin directed them from another plane.

Jordian looked at Juliana with question. What did he mean?

"Don't look with your eyes, look with your mind," Juliana explained to Jordian and tried to do as Merlin directed. "But what am I looking for, Merlin?" Juliana wanted to know.

Merlin started to laugh, "Me, of course. What else? Use your inner eye and see into another plane. You and Jordian met this time in your physical plane; then the two of you learned to move into the 'astral plane.' There are many energetic planes of existence, My Child. The two of you have learned to work them together, many times before. That is why it was so easy for Jordian to start this process with you. Work with your inner eye and look beyond. You know how, as you see the energies around people and plants, when you look beyond the physical. In a similar way, look beyond the astral and you will see me."

Now Juliana understood what Merlin was explaining. She had always been able to see beyond the physical confines and see the energetic fields he talked of when she travelled with him during their years together. She used that same awareness to go beyond this astral plane and she saw Merlin. "WOW, I did it," she exclaimed with delight, "I see you." But what a difference. On this plane, it was all about color; beams, rays, dancing colors. It was beautiful.

Jordian didn't like getting left behind like this. He could hear Juliana's thoughts and knew she had achieved what Merlin directed, but he was still back here. "Okay guys, can anyone help me with this, please? I seem to be stuck."

Merlin laughed, "In your last life, it was you who crossed over first and Juliana was asking for help. Be patient, Jordian. You have done this before in other life times. It is like making love, once you have learned to do it well you will never forget, even across life times. Just focus. Focus beyond what you see as if you are looking beyond the mountain in order to see the mountain."

While Merlin was helping Jordan, Juliana was playing with light and color. It was fascinating what you could do without the physical limitations. The colors were far more brilliant than anything she had ever seen on earth. You could actually see the composition of the light. "Hey I did it!" she heard Jordan exclaim, "WOW! Look at these colors. This is definitely beyond."

"Yes, it is," Merlin confirmed, "but the two of you need to learn how to use this wisely; the when and how. You have a lot more training to do. It is enough for one night."

"Oh, but I don't want to go just yet," Juliana told him. But in a moment, she was back in her bed. "How did you do that?" she wanted to know. She hadn't intended on coming back.

"You learned a long time ago, My Child. We get things done quicker and with greater ease when you follow my directions. Use that learning wisely," and with that, Merlin was gone.

Juliana and Jordan lay in bed looking at one another not sure what to say. There were no words for what they had experienced. Where was it? What were they supposed to learn to do with it? There were so many questions they each had but no answers.

"So, we have been together before," Jordan acknowledged. This was something he had a better ability to focus on. "I always thought we had, it was so easy when we met that day on the path. We worked in unison collecting wood and making our dinner, as if we had worked together many times before. It felt like I had always known you. It was almost as if you were an extension of me that I had just rediscovered. I didn't want to say anything because it was such a strange sensation for me and we had just met. I was so pleased when Merlin came to me during the night and told me what to say to you.

But now this puts it all into such a different perspective. We have been together and worked together before."

"Yes, yes," Juliana was still so excited, "and we have done this other stuff before too. Remember what Merlin said, 'there are many energetic planes of existence, My Child. And the two of you have learned to work them together, many times before. That is why it was so easy for Jordian to start this process with you.' Jordian, we have not only been together on this plane, but on many planes. That is why we work together so well, with everything. Oh, I do love you so."

She threw her arms around him and he laughed in delight. "Yes, apparently, we have and I love you too, My Lady. What are we to do with it? How does it benefit us to be able to travel together on different energetic planes? Does it give us the capacity to help others, more? I don't know. I am anxious to learn more."

They talked long into the night about what it all meant. And then before they knew it, the children ran in to wake them up. They were very excited; their eldest child, Nigel, had spotted a bear in the woods. Yes, it was morning, it had come too soon, and it demanded their full attention.

Chapter 24

Weird

Jordan and Jasmine loved their time together. It didn't matter what they were doing: socializing with friends; cooking together; researching; making love; showering together; or riding their bikes.

They often teased one another that they needed something to fight about. They had no idea how the other fought. They needed to make sure they each fought fairly and logically and effectively, before they could commit to getting married. They knew they did everything else together.

One night it happened again. They had just made love. It had started out very romantic and sweet and evolved into an intense passion. They were lying back on the bed, wiped out from their 'bed exercise'. Jordan reached out and took her hand and just held it without saying a word. All of a sudden they were both 'out of their bodies'. Right away she looked around for him, yes; he was out of his body too.

This time, the shock of it didn't propel them back into their bodies. Jasmine's scientific mind wanted to know what was going on. She motioned for him to stay. She tried to figure out her essence. She didn't have a physical body but there was more to her than just pure energy; she had form and so did he. She could see his form. "What the hell is going on?" she didn't realize she had said it out loud and as soon as she did, they were both back in their bodies.

"Okay, now that was really weird," he exclaimed looking around the room making sure he was back in his body and everything else was still normal.

"Yes, but what is it? What causes it? What are we made of when we do that?" the questions raced out of her mouth. She had questions but no answers.

They both just laid there on the bed, feeling the solidness of their bodies and the bed. Her mind was analyzing; talking out loud, she looked for patterns, "Both times we were here in your apartment; both times we were in your bed; both times we just finished making love," she rolled over and gave him a kiss, "and it was good."

He smiled; he loved that they could make love with so many different emotions and attitudes. They always seemed to be so in tune with whatever the tone of the moment was. She pulled him back to the present. "Think for a moment. What made sex different on these two occasions than on other occasions?" her mind was moving fast; analyzing, comparing, and doing a mental dance through all the variables.

"Okay, so let's think," she continued, "was it the tone of making love? What were we doing the first time it happened? We were a little drunk and we had started out laughing on the floor; then it became really hot and intense. It was like I couldn't get enough of you. Then we lay back on the bed wiped out." She remembered it in minute detail.

She had never experienced anything like it. He loved listening to her explain what they had done. It had been as intense for her as it had been for him. He loved it.

"I remember, you reached over and grabbed my hand and then, voila, that thing happened. That's what happened this time. We started out more romantic, but again it evolved into hot intense passion. We both fell back afterwards, and you reached out and took my hand. And again, viola, it happened. What is it about you taking my hand, when we are in that space, that makes it happen?" She rolled over and started drawing circles around his chest with a finger.

He loved it when she did that, it created a strange sensation in him. It was like an oxymoron, it made him quiver and at the same time felt so relaxing. "Do you have any idea, what that does to me?"

"What? What does what?" she was confused, wasn't he concentrating on what happened a few moments ago?

"Yes, I know we are trying to figure out how that weird experience happens. But then you rolled over and started drawing circles on my chest with your finger which got me side tracked. I love it when you do that. I love what it does to my body."

"We just had this phenomenal experience. And you are wrapped up in me drawing circles on your chest? Are you crazy?"

"Yes, I am crazy. I am crazy in love with you. And I love what you make happen in my body. And yes, that was a very strange experience that happened, again. Just being with you is a phenomenal experience." he motioned for her to follow him to the bathroom to get cleaned up while they talked. "What happens in my body, when you touch me? What happens in my head when I look at you? What happens in my nervous system when I anticipate seeing you? They are all phenomenal experiences and I really hope you have the same kind of phenomenal experiences in reaction to me."

She nodded agreement.

"What just happened now is a weird experience. And yes, I recognize you want to understand it and I can only imagine where our research is going to take us, but for right now, I am going to just let it rest. We both have to get up in a few hours and have busy days ahead of us. Making love was great; being out of our bodies was really weird; and all this talking is just making me more tired." They got back into bed. "What I want for us, right now, is to go to sleep. We will try to understand it in the morning. Can that work for you?"

She smiled at him as they rolled into their favorite sleeping position. She loved that their bodies just knew how to roll together. It was like they had done it for a lifetime, yet they had only been together for eight months. She knew he was tired and wanted to sleep, so she abided by his request. She would get up later, after he was asleep and do some research on the computer. She smiled lovingly at him. He was the best. He kissed her sweetly on the mouth and said he would see her in his dreams.

Jasmine planned on getting up and researching their 'weird' experience, but it didn't happen, instead she fell asleep right alongside Jordan.

She often knew she was dreaming when she was dreaming. She couldn't make it happen, it just happened, though never with intent.

Tonight, again, she knew she was dreaming. She was kneeling on the ground in a forested area looking for something. A plant, why was she looking for a plant? What plant was she looking for? Why would she be dreaming about looking for a plant? Then she remembered, she was looking for a plant for a medicinal formulation. Why wouldn't she just get the medicine out of the pharmacy? At that point she also recognized her clothes felt weird and she looked down at herself. No, these were definitely not her clothes. Okay, this was a dream. She was dreaming about herself being in a different era. In the dream, in the different era, she was a woman who looked for plants for medicinal purposes. She was an herbalist!

WOW! This was an interesting dream. She wanted to make sure she remembered this dream when she woke up. Someone was calling her. It was a man. In the dream she knew this man. She knew he was calling her, but her name was somehow different. He was calling Juliana not Jasmine. Okay, so it was a dream. She looked down the pathway for the man calling her. It was Jordan. Well, it didn't look like Jordan, but somehow, she knew it was. She called to him, to let him know where she was. He had a look in his eyes. She knew that look. It was the same look Jordan had when he would meet her somewhere. It was full of life and energy and a love that crosses over time.

And then she was awake and in her bed. Jordan was kissing her awake. He wanted to make love again before they got up and went to work.

Not this morning. Not for her. She wanted to remember the dream. She put a hand up motioning him to stop. "You wouldn't believe what happened to me last night."

He looked at her with a smirk on his face, "Oh yeah, I remember. We both ended up out of our bodies again. Believe me, I will be working right alongside you for the next few days trying to figure that out. But for now…" he put a hand out to cradle a breast and start making love to her.

But she put up a hand again, "Yeah, I know. Don't. Stop. Listen to me." She had never said no to their love making before. But this was important, and she didn't want to forget what happened in the dream.

He stopped. Was the infatuation over? She had never said no to him before. He rolled back, disappointed and hurt and rather frustrated.

"Listen to me," she pulled him back on his side again, "this is important, for me, for both of us. Something is happening here."

Well he thought something was going to happen, but it obviously wasn't what he had intended.

"I mean it, just listen for a minute. Do you ever have dreams where you know you are dreaming?" she didn't wait for his answer, "Well I do sometimes and last night I did. But it was different. I was on the ground looking for a plant for a medicinal herbal formulation, I think. I was in clothes from another time. Maybe medieval times, I'm not sure. Then you were calling my name. Except it wasn't you; but it was you. I mean, it didn't look like you, but I knew it was you. You were calling me Juliana instead of Jasmine," she paused to catch her breath.

"You were in a dream basically about you and me, in another time. You knew it was us, but we looked different and we had different names?" Jasmine nodded her head excitedly. It meant something, she just didn't know what. And after what happened last night, this was getting really exciting.

"And you think this is something important? Especially after the weird experience we had last night?" *Well okay, that is enough to lose a hard on over,*' he grimaced to himself. "Okay, I hear you. It is intriguing. But what do you want to make of it? Where can anyone go with something like that? And…" he waited for her to answer some of his questions.

"I don't know," she confessed, "but what if it does mean something? Have you ever thought about reincarnation? What if we were together in another life time? What if we have abilities we have already learned? What if we could go back and forth across lifetimes? What if we could learn better from past, I mean really past mistakes? This could be huge."

"Yes, it could. And it could just be a dream. Let's not get ahead of ourselves here. Let's just take this weird stuff one step at a time, or we might end up in an institution." He got out of bed and started walking to the ensuite. He obviously wasn't going to get any this morning, so they might as well start getting ready for work.

"Well you are right, it could all be just some crazy distortion of the mind. But what if it wasn't?" Jasmine quickly followed him into the bathroom.

"I might not be getting any this morning, but at least come have a shower with me so I can ravage that sexy body of yours."

Jasmine smiled and started to pull off the t-shirt she wore to bed, but Jordan stopped her. He wanted to pull it off for her. He might not get any in bed this morning, but he might get some in the shower. *'God I love this woman, craziness and all,'* he said to himself, although out loud, so she could hear this thoughts. He wanted her to know how he loved her.

He slowly pulled off her t-shirt with a raised eyebrow and a smile of satisfaction. One hand went to cradle one of her lovely breasts as he teased it out from under her t-shirt. Moments later, he exposed the other one with an already taunt nipple, to his waiting mouth. He let go long enough to dance her into the shower. He handed her a bar of soap to work his body and she started to giggle.

"Are you attempting to wash my body or are you attempting to entice it?" she questioned with a knowing look. It was obvious what he was up to and she didn't have what it took to stop him, this time. Between spitting out gulps of unwanted shower water and laughing like children, they were actually able to make love. It was a small shower which made it a very awkward entanglement. But they came out washed, rinsed and satiated with smiles on their faces.

"If I can't get you one way, I will get you another," he said with a smug look on his face and a twinkle in his eye. "And yes, I agree with you, your dream does seem rather weird AND, yes, it kind of walks, sort of, hand in hand with the weirdness that happened last night." She had given him what he wanted and now he was more than willing to give her what she wanted. "So why don't we make a date for tonight? We will just order in pizza and spend the evening researching this weird stuff on our computers. Maybe there is something out there to will help us understand what is going on with us, My Wanton Witch."

"Oooh, now I am a Wanton Witch. I am not sure if that sounds like a good thing or a bad thing. But yes, let's do it."

Chapter 25

The research begins

It was an easy day for Jasmine, well, relatively speaking anyway. She couldn't wait to get home and start researching. She didn't dare tell anyone at work what had happened. They would commit her to the psych ward for sure.

As soon as she finished her shift, she phoned Jordan to see if he had finished on time too. He was sorry; he had a big client he had to stay with for another hour. He would be late but would make it for a late dinner if that was okay. She could order the pizzas and have everything ready, so they could start researching as soon as he got home. *'She'll be researching as soon as she walks in the door, forget about waiting for me,'* he laughed to himself.

'Home' now meant Jordan's place. Jasmine had moved in after their return from the 'Ribbon Cutting' ceremony in Tanzania. The hospital let her have another week because they again thought it would be great advertising. They wanted pictures of her at the ribbon cutting, preferably cutting the ribbon. So, they gave her the week off.

It was a fun trip. Hawkeye showed her his new bachelor pad and introduced her to all the current volunteers. She asked if he was going to stay and 'run the ship,' but he didn't think so. This place would now be relatively easy for someone else to run. On the other hand, the makeshift tarp sites were a lot harder and there were fewer people like him willing to run those kinds of 'ships'. So, he had committed to staying till the hospital was 'up and running'. Then he would probably apply for another 'tarp'.

She gave him a hug, saying, "What would the world do without people like you? You truly are 'one of a kind'."

She helped the current volunteers organize the remaining dispensary and the emergency room equipment and Pharmacia. Most of the move had already been done, there was little for her to help with.

She and Jordan had loved the experience of going back to where they first connected. It felt like it had been a lifetime ago, when in reality it had only 7 weeks. The initial 3-week plan had been postponed because some government official had wanted to be there for pictures.

Hawkeye loaned them his jeep and a guide, and they were able to tour some surrounding areas before they returned home with Jordan laughingly suggesting they call this their 'pre-honeymoon'. She agreed and told him she hoped he appreciated all the time and effort she put into organizing their 'pre-honeymoon'. They were always laughing, and she was so glad they shared the same type of 'goofy humor'. It made life so much easier. While on their 'pre-honeymoon' they agreed she would move into his place and rent out her apartment. She had a good rate on the mortgage and could rent it for much more, so it made sense to rent it out and make money on it. This would also provide extra income for when Jordan decided to open his own office.

Tonight, Jasmine didn't mind his coming home late. She could race home, have a shower, order the pizzas and start getting the research organized. During the day, she organized a spread sheet in her mind with the different questions she wanted answered. Each section provided her with space to put in data and research and references. She hoped to have it done before Jordan walked in. And she did.

Even the pizzas worked out great. They arrived about 10 minutes before he did. She had ordered two small ones; a Mediterranean or her and a Meat Eaters for him. She put them in the oven to keep them warm. The plates and napkins were out along with a knife and fork for her. She always preferred to eat pizza with a knife and fork.

The Excel spreadsheet was finished, and she was already looking things up. There was a lot of information about "OBEs" or out of body experiences. *How come everyone else knows about this stuff and I don't?* she questioned out loud.

There was a ton of information on reincarnation and people who claimed they had gone into past lives. The research was fascinating, and she had already down loaded a few books.

There was a famous psychiatrist who used hypnosis to take people into past lives to heal relationships and other issues. She downloaded the books he published. His write up, for the first book, explained he had no idea what was happening to a client who kept going into these other personalities. Was she a 'Multiple Personality Disorder;' a 'Borderline Personality Disorder;', or was she psychotic? He tested the client for different types of psychosis but found none. He had no background in reincarnation and could find nothing in medical research. When he went beyond the confines of Conventional Medicine, he had found a ton of information. It had taken several years before he was willing to publish his book. Understandably he didn't want to have to deal with peer criticism. She knew she was up against the wall. Western medicine was hugely based in the old Newtonian sciences. This stuff was definitely out in 'left field'.

She was deep into all of it when Jordan came in. "Hi Hon. How did it go with the clients?" she looked up from her work.

"As you know, they are the last big project before I leave, so I want to make a really good impression, so I start with a good reputation. Yeah me!" he said with a 'thumbs up'. "There was a snag we needed to work through, and as luck would have it, I was able to turn it into something that worked even better," he beamed with his success. It had obviously been a good day for him.

Jasmine stood up and shook his hand then gave him a hug and a kiss. She handed him the glass of wine she poured for him 10 minutes before. "I am not surprised. Aren't you the best creative architectural engineer in the world?" she praised him with a love and devotion he was getting very addicted to. It was so different being with someone who loved and admired his work, as opposed to his family who lacked any kind of appreciation for his talents and thought he was a 'flake'.

"Well, I would say it is kind of on par, with the best physician the world has to offer, wouldn't you say?" he returned in kind. He was so proud of her work and how good she was at it AND she had the compassionate bed side manner so many physicians lacked. As with everything she did, she went way beyond what was required.

"Go get into some comfys and I will put out the pizzas and show you what I've got so far."

They spent the night researching all kinds of stuff; trying to find good research; weeding out all the hocus pocus kind of stuff; until they actually found some really good interesting studies.

They found Ruth Montgomery's work and Dr. Raymond Moody's work, read some Dr. Brian Weiss's books, and so much more. It was fascinating. Why don't they teach us anything about this stuff in med school?" she wanted to know, "It is all about the human condition, but we don't know any of it. It's as bad as with all the nutritional and herbal stuff. We know so little, when we are supposed to know so much. Although with that stuff, they call it 'alternative medicine' and then tell us there isn't any support for it. Yet when I look it up on the internet in the PLoS, that stands for the People's Library of Science; or PubMed, that's all the peer review medical studies and articles; there are all kinds of journals that have a ton of really good research. It doesn't make any sense. I feel like I need to go back to school and learn all the really good important stuff now.

You know, in Western societies, we eliminated anything that could be considered magic or folklore and tried to replace it with real 'scientific' experimentation and results. But we not only lost humanity in the process, but I think now, Western science is just another money maker with little substance to it, especially in medical research." Jasmine complained with an element of excitement as they were getting ready for bed. "I wonder if we can make that OBE happen again tonight."

"Hey, I'm gain, if that means I get some again tonight. In fact, I have a suggestion, how about we make love every morning and every night and three times on Saturdays and Sundays until we figure out how we can do this thing on command. And of course, once we figure it out, then we have to practice, practice, practice to get it down pat," he committed to her as he climbed on top of her.

"Aren't you the committed one?" she acknowledged his dedication, "Willing to go above and beyond the call of duty in the name of research. How could I ever say no to such diligence?"

They made love and then relaxed back on their backs. He reached out to hold her hand, but it didn't happen. They talked for a while about what they could have done differently. What they had researched. And eventually they rolled into their favorite positions and fell asleep.

Chapter 26

Opening Ceremonies

Both of their schedules were very busy. Her hospital routine was always busy. They needed more physicians, but the hospital wouldn't hire any more. There was always conflicts with budgets and the insurance coverages and a host of other things Jasmine just had no time for. She went to the meetings, only because she was required to. She did her job, often putting in overtime, and loved her work. She really did not want anything to do with the finances. She understood the hospital needed finances and needed to work with a budget. The hospital had to pay for the drugs, the different types of scanning equipment, and wages for everyone from those who washed floors to the medical specialists. She knew all that. She just didn't want to be a part of it. It took away from the pleasure of being able to help people.

Jordan's busy-ness came from him opening his new office. It was another fun 'Ribbon Cutting' Ceremony. They even sent an invitation to Hawkeye. They didn't expect him to actually attend, but thought it was nice gesture. There were, however, a lot of friends and colleagues from both of their professions, who did attend.

The highlight of the ceremony was when Hawkeye did show up. He had given them no advance warning he was coming so it was a huge surprise and it meant so much to both of them. Jasmine had tears in her eyes and Jordan kept going over to Hawkeye and giving him another hug. His own family chose not to come. It didn't meet their criterion of success or achievement. Yet Hawkeye, a man he admired so much, was willing to travel half way around the world to be there for him. Apparently, Hawkeye needed to come to the US for some fund-raising programs and did some fancy foot work, so he could be at the 'Ribbon Cutting Ceremony'. What a day.

Chapter 27

Her Dreams

Due to Jordan's developing reputation as a creative engineering genius, plus his work with 'Green' architecture, he had clients right away. They were small and only a few, but it was enough to keep the doors open without having to draw funds from any of their other income sources. When he wasn't working with clients he was researching with Jasmine. There had been a few more experiences of suddenly being out of body. It always seemed to happen when they were together, though they still had no idea how or why it happened. They wanted to learn how to control it and work with it.

They experimented with different types of meditation they had come across to see if that would influence their experience. What they found was, meditation worked wonders for their stress levels, it allowed their minds to think more clearly. It was like the meditation took away a film from the mind, so their thoughts were clearer; thinking was easier; and problem solving was more creative. But it hadn't yet had any impact on their 'weird experiences'. They worked at it more and more frequently struggling to learn what it was that allowed them to move out of their bodies.

Then one night in a dream, Jasmine met a woman called Juliana. Juliana told her she needed to learn to take control of the 'out of body' experience. Jasmine agreed with her and asked her if she could tell her how to do that. Juliana took Jasmine's hand, "Be with me." Juliana directed her. Somehow, Jasmine knew what that meant and all of a sudden understood how to take control. It was like Juliana shared the experience with Jasmine as opposed to explaining to Jasmine how to do it. Whatever it was, now Jasmine understood and couldn't wait to wake up and tell Jordan. But Juliana had other plans and she took control of the dream. Jasmine didn't seem to have issue with that, which seemed odd to her. She felt like she knew this woman. She trusted her. *'It must be a dream companion I have dreamt about before,'* she thought to herself.

Juliana had read her mind and responded, "It is actually more than that; you will learn everything in good time." Jasmine obviously had no idea what that meant but was willing to be patient.

Then Juliana guided Jasmine over to a patio like area with a table and chairs. There was a cup of tea waiting for Jasmine. It was a kind of herbal type tea Jasmine was not familiar with, but it was nice. Then Juliana talked with Jasmine about many things. Jasmine kept thinking to herself, *'Remember everything she says, this is important.'*

She was so excited about the dream when she woke up. Jordan was still asleep, so, she tried to do what Juliana had taught in the dream. She did it; she was up at the ceiling looking down at Jordan. She went back down into her body, then up again. Yes, she definitely could do it. Should she tell Jordan she could? She wanted him to have a similar kind of dream. Maybe she should just tell him all the other stuff first? She didn't know. It was Saturday morning and they

135

could laze in bed. She drew circles on Jordan's chest to wake him up. She couldn't wait to tell him about the dream.

"Okay My Lady, are you asking for trouble?" he grinned with one eye open.

"I had another dream. In order words, Jordan, don't get a hard on. Wake up and listen to me. I am so excited and can't wait to tell you about one of my crazy dreams."

Then," he drawled to make a point, "if you are lucky, I mean really lucky, you might get some playtime both in the bed and then again in the shower?"

Jasmine laughed at him, "Okay you kind of nailed it and added on some extra. Seeing how it's you, I guess I could try really hard to accommodate you. The average gal might not be able to handle it and, it will take a lot out of me, so you will have to be extra special to me all day," she bartered.

"Extra special, that means I should provide you with some extra special 'afternoon delight' and then after a romantic dinner restaurant, come home to pleasure your sexy body again?" he teased.

"Ha, you couldn't get it up four times in one day," she laughed, "but then again, yeah, you probably could," she conceded.

He grabbed her and pulled her down to him, "It's a deal then?"

"Well, only if you listen to me first," she so wanted to tell him about her dream.

He pulled the covers over his head and spoke to his member, "Did you hear that young man, you are simply going to have to wait till My Lady tells me about her dreams?"

Jasmine loved his playfulness and was always more than happy to join in. She pulled up the sheets and stuck her head under the sheets as well. "Now don't go way you 'al, you hear?" she said to his boys with a southern drawl. She then pulled the sheets up over him and swung a leg over his. She moved up and over him and sitting on top of him, she pinned him down to the bed. "And you, My Lord, you need to lay back and listen to me. I have so much to tell you."

"Well I tell you, My Sweet Lady, I would much rather you straddled this buck when you are under the sheets rather than over them. But yes, you now have my full attention," he kept his eyes pinned to hers as if she had his full attention, but let his fingers draw patterns up her bare legs and under her nightie obviously intent on finding her sacred spot. She knew she was obviously not going to get her story in before they made love. She was enjoying the playfulness too much. She started to hum the strip tease song and very enticingly brought her nightgown up to one of her breasts and let it slide out enough to give him a show. Then brought her nightie back down and slowly brought it up the other side to reveal another taunt nipple, then brought it back down again.

"You Wanton Witch, you," he grinned enjoying the entertainment.

Continuing with the song, she rocked seductively on him until she felt him get hard, "Well that didn't take long," she acknowledged. Then she pulled one leg up and to the side, allowing her to pull the sheet out from between them pulling her leg back into place and straddling him again. His member quickly found its wet and ready partner. Their love making was fun and playful and entertaining. They laughed and played and teased one another; as usual it didn't take too long before her body started to vibrate. She came several times until he simply couldn't hold back any more and they exploded, still laughing.

Jordan rolled out of bed and bent down to pick her up. He moved his hands under her fanny and she wrapped her arms around him. As he pulled her up, she wrapped her legs around him and he walked the two of them into the shower giggling. It was a maneuver to get them through the door, but they managed. The laughter continued into the shower where they tickled and teased and tormented one another's bodies with delight. Eventually, they were satiated and after rinsing one last time and getting a last 'stroke', they came out of the shower.

"Okay, now tell me tell me your dream."

"Forget it, I'm not telling you now. I've had to endure waiting this long, now you can make me breakfast and I will share it with you over breakfast."

He grabbed her towel and pulled her roughly to him as if angry with her. "Well, if that's the way you want to be, You Wanton Witch, I will take advantage of your sexy body, one last time," he finished with a twinkle in his eye.

He allowed the bath sheets to drop and pulled her naked body to his. Wrapping one arm around her and allowing his other hand to stroke through her wet hair, he gently covered her mouth with his. It was a long lingering kiss that spoke of the love he had for her, "Just think, we get to do this for a lifetime."

Her arms wrapped around him. One reaching down to grab onto a wet cheek while the other just held him close. Eventually they released each other, and she asked, "Have you had enough, at least for a few hours?"

"Oh, I don't know, but I will let you know."

They dressed and went out to make breakfast. He was great at making omelets. She set the table and put in toast while he performed his breakfast magic. When they were seated at the kitchen table and ready to eat, he asked again, "Okay so what was the dream about that you couldn't wait to wake me up for?"

"Remember, the last time when I had that dream when I knew I was dreaming? Well it was like that. It was even in the same place and time I was in before. The other woman is Juliana. She is an herbalist from that time and place and apparently known for her capacity to heal people. She invited me over to their home, a short way from the garden. In fact, I think the garden was at the back of her home. She had a cup of herbal tea already made. She told me you and I are another version of her and her husband. His name is Jordian and he also builds and creates. From time to time they cross planes and try to connect with us. That is when we end up out of body. They know we are researching how to do it. And they want to help."

"And I take it from all of your excitement; you think this dream is some sort of actuality rather than just a dream? Aren't we taking this a little far? I mean really, how can you, be both you and her? And how can one aspect of us travel across time like that. I mean this is really sci-fi kind of stuff, don't you think? You are a doctor for heaven's sake, Jasmine. Surely this is just some part of the mind being creative during sleep; a part of the mind that is always searching for answers?"

"Well, there's more. I asked her if Jordian could come to you in a dream and talk with you. I know how far-fetched this all sounds to you; and I how real it seems to me. I thought if you experienced one of these dreams it might become just as real for you?"

"So now you want me to believe this Jordian guy, who is really me but lives in another time and place, is going to come and talk with me in a dream?" he started to laugh, "There is nothing like going way out into left field. I don't really think that is going to happen any time soon."

"Well, let's not draw too many conclusions too fast. If we are open to it, Jordian may come to you tonight."

" Oh Shit. Do I have any say in this matter?"

"Well I don't really know, but I would like you to be open to it. My suggestion is we have a really great day today. Take a break from doing research and just go out and have fun. We can take our bikes and go for a picnic, or a hike or a drive. I don't care what we do, but I don't want to be sitting around all day dwelling on it. We need to go out and have fun."

"You're on; sounds like a great plan for the day, but I doubt whether I am going to be having one of your dreams tonight." Jasmine just grinned, she had faith in Juliana.

Chapter 28

Let's Just Have Fun

After they cleaned up the breakfast dishes, they made themselves a picnic lunch, put their bikes on the bike hitch on Jordan's car, grabbed some beach towels, just in case, and drove out to the Mystic Lakes. It was a beautiful day. The sun was bright but not warm enough for sun bathing. Parking their car, they got on their bikes and went for a ride along the beach. There was a gentle breeze in the air enticing the waves to gently dance against the shoreline singing their songs.

They rode for over an hour before deciding to stop at some park benches and eat the apples they had brought along. The waves twinkled in the sunlight. The breeze sang in the tree leaves. It was a perfect day.

"Remember when we were in Africa? Sitting under that hot UN tarp and savoring a glass of rationed water? Now look at us here. What a difference. Have you thought about when we might go on another project?" he asked as he took another bite out of his apple.

"Yes, I surely do remember. That is where I think I fell in love with you. Or maybe it was when you showed me the bachelor suites behind the physicians' offices in the hospital. I don't really know when I fell in love with you. It was like it was just always there. Not like 'love at first site', but more of a simple knowing I was too scared to acknowledge. I was so hurt when you weren't there the first week I was back. And then when I saw you standing in front of my office door with the balloons and the orchids, I knew I had fallen hard, but I didn't want you to know."

He laughed, "I was trying to hide my heart with the orchids. I thought being you were a physician, you would be able to tell how hard it was beating, and I felt like a silly teen age boy. God, my heart ached for you till you returned. Actually, it still does, it goes into a dance every day when I leave the office, just to know I am going to see you when I get home. I hope that lasts for a life time."

"I didn't know that. Well I will let you in on a little secret. My heart starts to beat as soon as I get organized to leave my office at the end of the day too. I know I will be seeing you and all is well with the world. What if it even lasts across life times? Ever think? After the conversation I had in my dreams last night, this reincarnation stuff is becoming more and more real to me. I have been researching quantum physics lately and when you start looking at string theory and 11 dimensions and moving outside the five dimensions and beyond space and time and all that stuff, it really starts to open up doors of possibility. It starts to make room for this stuff we have been researching lately."

"I know what you mean; I have been looking at that stuff too, trying to make use of it in my designs. It's all fascinating. It makes you really start to appreciate the old saying, 'the more you know, the more you know you don't know'.

Maybe the reason I am anxious and don't know if I want to have that dream tonight, is because there are too many unknowns for my little mind to deal with. What if it destroys our relationship somehow; our connection with what we think of as reality; or causes some other difficulty?"

"Both times I have connected in my dreams; there has been a peaceful acceptance. I haven't been pushed or forced. It seems to leave me with a kind of acceptance, I never had before. Besides the ability to learn how to move outside of our bodies, there is another aspect I am drawn too."

"Oh no, not more; I don't know if I can handle it?" he teased trying to light up the conversation.

"Well stop whining and listen. This Juliana person, whether she is another part of me or a part of me in another lifetime or whatever it is, she is an herbalist. She apparently has a great reputation for healing people across the land; well, whatever that land might be. She told me people spend days and even 'moons' travelling to see her, and she heals them. It triggers that part of me that wants to learn about food and nutrition and herbs and spices and REAL medicines that really eliminate the problems without harming the body."

"Uh oh, now you are really getting into witch craft. You are going to be burned at the stake," he teased.

"Well in the physicians' world I might. But whether you believe in some kind of evolution or some kind of creation, either way the body was designed to work with nature. Whether it is the receptors on the cells receiving compounds or the enzymes used to metabolize medicines, it just makes more sense that our bodies were designed to work with REAL medicine rather than synthetic laboratory man made stuff."

"Okay, but isn't it the 'real stuff' that allowed the body to go sideways in the first place? Isn't that why you use the synthetic stuff, to help the body get back on track?"

"That is certainly what we were taught in med school. I wonder if we were actually taught the right things in med school; I mean ultimately, the majority of my job is to push pills for Big Pharma. Is that really what a good physician should be doing? If I were really a good physician, I should know what toxins the body needs to get rid of. I should know what foods and herbs can help the body to get rid of those toxins. If the body needs nutrients because it is deficient in something, shouldn't I be able to identify the nutrients and help the person learn what foods contain those nutrients, then make sure they get the nutrient or nutrients? We keep hearing how everything is so toxic which must be terribly difficult for the body. Rather than giving the body more toxic synthetic compounds, shouldn't I really be giving them a prescription for the foods, herbs and nutrients the body requires to heal? I think, as physicians, we got lost along the way. We got conned into believing man knew better than nature. How incredibly arrogant. If man really was smarter than nature, then how come we keep learning more and more about how many of our drugs are failing more and more of the time; or how much of medical research is based on false assumptions."

He knew these questions haunted her in her practice. He just had no way of helping her resolve them. Maybe this

145

dream person might. "So, this woman in the dreams, the one that is you but isn't you, can she help you resolve your dilemmas?"

"I don't know. But I think she might have some answers for me. I can't wait to talk with her again."

Chapter 29

His Dream

The rest of the day was fun. They rode their bikes back to the car, took out their picnic lunch and a blanket, and had a picnic in the park beside the lake. It was a gentle day. No pressures. No business. They finished their lunch and walked down to the path along the lake, then walked in the other direction to buy ice cream cones. Eventually, they came home and had their promised 'afternoon delight'.

After a quick shower, they dressed for dinner and went for a nice Thai dinner in a romantic restaurant with quiet background music. There was no dance floor, but they enjoyed a lovely relaxing evening. Their conversations meandered through possible projects they might venture into around the world; what their dream home might look like; and how he saw his business developing. They discussed all kinds of different topics involving the two of them while avoiding the dream topic.

Returning home, Jasmine asked if he wanted to meditate before going to bed. He knew she was thinking it might be helpful for the dream he was supposed to have tonight. He was still apprehensive about it and thought a meditation might calm his mind down and so he agreed. He even allowed their promise to make love skip by; he was definitely apprehensive.

Then when he was in the meditation, he heard a voice, "Do not worry. This will be good." It was kind of strange. He didn't come to with a start, but rather, it created the same type of calm and acceptance Jasmine had spoken of. It was weird and yet it was okay. They finished their meditations and crawled into bed. He didn't say anything to Jasmine about the voice.

When they rolled into their favorite position, she said, "Sweet dreams." And tonight, it had a whole different meaning than it usually did.

He laughed and responded, "Well, who knows, maybe I will see you there too?" He figured it would take him a while to get to sleep even with the meditation, but he slipped off quickly. Jasmine woke up several times during the night both anxious for him and wanting to know if he had any dreams yet.

Jordan was now aware he was dreaming. '*Well this is interesting,*' he thought to himself, '*this is what Jasmine means when she says she knows she is dreaming. Okay, so far so good.*' He looked around him; he didn't recognize where he was, but it didn't seem unusual or out of time and place. He moved around getting a feel for it. What was he supposed to be doing? Nothing seemed to be going on. He was just walking along a pathway that could have been in any national park. Then he rounded a bend and now he was definitely, somewhere different. '*Okay, so where is this place?*' he asked out loud but to himself, as there was no one else there.

"This is another time and place." a voice said beside him, "This is where Jasmine comes."

Jordan turned and looked at the man beside him. He was a good-looking man but obviously from another era. '*Not a bad looking dude.*' Jordan said to himself.

"And you are also 'not a bad looking dude'." the man responded as if he could read Jordan's thoughts. "Yes, we can communicate telepathically on this level. And yes, I am you in another life time. My name is Jordian. Names are similar and so are the physiques, although universally speaking, that is rather unusual. Come here and take a seat. I have been waiting for you to be ready for this introduction. My wife, in this lifetime, is called Juliana. And yes, it is a strange concept when we are limited with physical perceptions. But yes, our beings; our energy; our minds; our soul; or whatever you want to call it, can cross both time and place. You and I are actually one in the same, but we have manifested in different lifetimes. You and your wife have been developing this ability in various lifetimes. It is one of the reasons you have such a deep love for one another. You have 'a love that crosses time'. And with that love you have also developed this other ability."

"Okay, if I am to accept this is all a weird dimension of reality and not some strange psychotic delusion, then explain to me what benefit it is to anyone?" his pragmatic mind wanted to know.

"A very good question, it allows us to help the 'true self'; to learn more effectively what we have already learned in another time. For instance, you are an architect and I have already travelled much and have learned and created many designs. Rather than wait to learn all that again, in the lifetime you are currently in, I will help you learn. You can travel across time and access what you have already learned in another lifetime and build on it. Many people do this without realizing it. That is when we call them a 'natural'; or they think they have woken up with a great idea, when in fact, they simply accessed it from another lifetime. When you have developed enough 'spiritually' shall we say, then you can do this with intent and purpose and gain so much more. You and Jasmine have been working to develop this ability since you lived in the ancient Ayurveda times in India. You were both part of the Brahmi class back then and were given special lessons in developing our 'spiritual' abilities, which is what the Brahmi were known for. I am sure you, or us, however you want to see it, have also experienced many lives prior to the Ayurveda life times, but I have not gone back further than yet. We actually have a guide teaching us both on the physical plane and on other planes. We lovingly call him Merlin. During her youth Juliana coined that name for him when he was a very loving mentor, teacher and friend to her. He has actually been with us for a very much longer time, not just in this lifetime."

"Will I meet this Merlin?" it was one simple question amongst a multitude of questions Jordan had, but where to start?"

"Yes, you will. Merlin is helping us train, in our lifetime, by helping us to connect with you."

"So, you can go forward to the future as well?" Jordan took a deep breath. Goodness, this was really heavy-duty stuff.

"You are just learning about 'quantum physics' in your lifetime. The scientists still don't have it quite right, but they are getting there. Basic quantum physics teaches you, you

150

can go past our five dimensions here and through a multitude of dimensions. When you leave the first five dimensions, you also leave time and space. People are confusing, some call this the third-dimension others think of it as having 5 dimensions, i.e., height, depth, width, time and space. Anyways, when you move into this level of beingness, you can move forward or backward in time, because there is no time. Time and space are no longer limitations. There are many souls who throughout the ages have learned these lessons. In the past, they were given a variety of names from Shamans and Healers to Cross Overs and the like. But in the time era that you live, most of this knowledge has been lost, at least in Western societies, or at best considered hocus pokey. Is that the term?"

"You mean, hocus pocus or hokey pokey?" Jordan corrected, "Yeah, you are right. I am still apparently learning this stuff and still having a difficult time coming to terms with it. Are we supposed to go through some special training? Am I supposed to be doing something during the day to prepare for your visits or something?"

Jordian started to laugh, "No, this is not the kind of school you went to. Juliana and I are working towards connecting with you more and more, both for our benefit and for yours. After all, we are all one. There is so much to learn, you will be amazed. You get to a point where you can't get enough of it, but then you have to find a way to balance this with your day to day life. You will see, my friend. I think this is enough for one night. You have a lot to assimilate into your thinking, so I will say, 'till next time'."

Jordan woke up with a start, *'Holy shit!"* he said to himself, although out loud.

Jasmine was wide awake and waiting to hear what happened to him. She had a big grin on her face. He obviously had a dream. She couldn't wait to hear what happened.

He opened his eyes to see her lying on her side watching him. He put up a hand to indicate to her not to ask him anything, "No not yet. Give me a moment."

Jordan needed to get all the information organized in his head before he could talk about it. He got up and went into the ensuite. He went to the bathroom, washed his hands, then brushed his teeth. What other mundane normal things could he do to help him organize his thoughts? Had he even slept? The dream experience seemed to have taken the whole night, but they said dreams were usually very short lived, we only perceive them to be longer. *'Well that's the least of my concerns,'* he said to himself as he tried to remember all he had been told in the dream. He walked into the bedroom, and again held up his hand motioning Jasmine not to ask or say anything. He got back into bed and just laid there with his thoughts turning, crashing and jumping all over the place.

Jasmine was delighted. His dream had a huge impact on him. Now he might appreciate how she felt yesterday, when all he wanted to do was to make love and she needed to talk. She knew Jordan operated differently than her. She talked to organize her thoughts; he organized his thoughts, so he could talk. He was obviously doing a lot of organizing. She could impatiently be patient, she laughed to herself.

"Okay so this it." he paused, "Geez, it seemed like insanity and at the same incredibly ingenious. Yeah, okay, this is it," he repeated himself, "I met Jordian who is Juliana's husband. Supposedly you and I are Juliana and Jordian. We have spent many lifetime's training, including special training back in India when we were Brahmins, or Ayurvedic something or other, or something. Someone, or something, called Merlin is also there to help with the training. We do this work, so we can learn from other lifetimes without having to do the training all over again. But we can move both forward and backward in time when we move out of the five dimensions. Is that how you have it figured?" he asked with an expression of incredibility.

"Yeah, that kind of sounds like what she told me." Jasmine agreed, "How do you feel about it?" she wanted to know.

"Wow! That was a lot to take in in one night. It sounds so crazy; but so, did the world being round instead of flat; so, did the air being full of microbes we couldn't see; or, or, or...

I am glad today is Sunday. I think the two of us need to sit in front of our computers and take a different route than where we were going before. Wow!" he said again.

"I love it." she laughed, "Just think, you wouldn't let me talk yesterday, before you ravished my body; then at breakfast you thought I was a lunatic; and now you have caught the bug. The joke is on you, bud!" she leaned over and kissed him. It felt so good to be back on the same page. It opened so many possibilities in their lives. She was the happy camper this morning wanting to laugh and have fun, now he was the serious one, but she knew how to get him going.

She lifted the sheet and peered under it, "Hey guys, anyone 'up' down there? Interested in some extra-curricular activities before we start to study? Yup, definitely see some activity." She turned the radio on and it accommodated her by providing some good hip dance music. She stood up on the bed and started to do another strip tease. Though she had a t-shirt and briefs on, she made it as much fun as she could. She worked the pillows and the sheets and made him laugh and finally came back down and straddled him like yesterday, although today there was no sheet to remove and she didn't have anything left on. He loved it.

"Okay, my Wanton Witch, you know me well. Come give me all you can."

They made love again. This time however, it evolved from a Burlesque strip performance into a gentle loving, slow and deep. It was a love that had already 'gone across time'.

Chapter 30

Learning Across Time

As they learned to travel, so did she learn about herbs, he about energy, and them about reality.

It didn't take long for Jordan and Jasmine to learn from Jordian and Juliana. First, they learned to move in and out of their bodies with intent and purpose; then to communicate telepathically more effectively outside their dreams; followed by a capacity to move in and out of more dimensions. It allowed Jordan to discover various techniques used throughout history that he could transform into different 'Green' effects for todays' homes and hospitals. He enjoyed working with Jordian who had travelled to some interesting places and came up with some very unique designs himself.

They worked on creating hospitals in places that wouldn't normally have the access to bring in the utilities. They developed plans, so they wouldn't have to rely on inaccessible utility services. Jordan just had to figure out a way to market the plans.

Juliana worked with Jasmine teaching her about all the different plants and herbs Merlin had taught her. Then Juliana would do research in the present and identify the herbal compounds considered medicinal and explore how they worked. They formed quite the team, and both loved it.

She collected as much information as possible. She was not allowed to use all the phenomenal information at work, but she could use the information when she worked on the international projects with Jordan.

One night, Jordian threw them a curve ball. The four of them planned to meet to work and share and study as they regularly did. This time, however, when Jasmine and Jordan showed up to work, there was another couple with Jordian and Juliana. Jordian and Juliana stood there shocked. There had never been anyone else; they hadn't even met Merlin yet. Who were these people?

Juliana had a big smile on her face, "We thought it was time you met another set of who we are. Please meet your former East Indian selves, this is Jasmini and Janardan. They were the first two we met, and we thought it was a good time for the two of you to meet them as well.

Apparently, Janardan and Jasmini knew all about Jordan and Jasmine. It was a strange concept; one part of the self could know about another part of the self in a different time and place, yet another part of the self-had no idea. Jordan turned to look at Jasmine, was this ever going to end? It was like they led two entirely separate lives. One, where they lived a 'normal' life, within the limited five dimensional perception of reality, pretending to believe in the normal concepts everyone else believed were reality. Then, there was this entirely separate life, where none of the normal rules of life applied. Jordan took Jasmine's hand and they walked towards the seat Jordian was motioning for them to sit down on.

Merlin appeared out of nowhere. Juliana stood up, "I know you. You were my study guide in university. You look so much older now."

"Yes, My Dear. You are correct. I worked with you and helped you gain what you needed from med school and helped you learn how to question what they were teaching."

Jordan looked at her, "You have to be kidding? He helped you? He helped me too. Oh my, is there anything that isn't an illusion in our reality? It seems like life is a very strange convolution of totally misunderstood concepts."

"You are right as well, Jordan. All of the life on earth is an illusion. Only those with the most developed abilities understand what an illusion it all is. It is what the old gurus and sages used to say, 'all life is an illusion that you create'. Once again, many are coming to the awareness that you really are in charge of your life. The Laws of Manifestation, as they are currently presented in your lifetime, are a little misleading. There is an aspect of truth to them, but in reality, they go much deeper than anyone actually understands. Let's all sit down for a bit and understand what is really going on."

"'*Really*' going on? I am beginning to think that word is an oxymoron in and of itself. Nothing is as it seems. The more we are shown, and the more we explore these different dimensions, the more nothing is ever *really* as we thought it was. Reality itself is an illusion." Jordan tried to explain his frustration.

"In a sense you are right." Merlin acknowledged. "Let's go back for a moment to give this night context. This is the first time the three aspects of both of you have come together AND come together with me." Merlin looked around for confirmation. "First off, let's clarify who I am. I have been known by many names throughout history. Janardan and Jasmini knew me as Babaji. I am well known throughout Eastern cultures as 'the one who comes and goes but never dies'. I am fondly known by Juliana and Jordian as Merlin, known throughout Western cultures as a magician, a romancer and a warrior depending on the era. I am known by Jasmine and Jordan as a study partner in university. Call me what you will, it is all me. For now, let's stay with Merlin, simply because I loved the way Juliana decided to name me.

So, what makes tonight special? Tonight, we are going to move further outside time and space. We will do so, so we are not limited by any dimension, for all we need to re-learn. Yes, re-learn. You see, the two of you have been around for eons. Not just here on earth, but through many different 'realities' if you want; planes of existence; whatever you want to call it. We are going to pull some of that understanding back into your awareness. Let's start with the physical world. We are taught the physical world, and all that is in it, is solid and the more solid or concrete something is, the more real it is. When in fact, the more 'solid' something is, the less reality it actually holds. You see, the senses themselves are an illusion. They are a very restrictive form of sensory perception. Many civilizations on earth teach if we can see, feel, or touch something, meaning if we can use our physical senses to experience something, it must be real. If it is beyond the physical senses, then it is not real especially since Descartes re-introduced scientific thinking back into Western civilization. Noticed I said re-introduced. Questioning, defining, testing, and observing perceived reality was not a new concept. It has been used numerous times throughout different civilizations and throughout earth history. What they thought was solid, actually isn't; air, water, soils, plants, even things as hard and solid as rocks they are learning, once again, are full of microbes. Sometimes these microbes are beneficial to humans, sometimes not, and sometimes it will depend on the individual whether the given microbe is a benefit or a detriment.

What couldn't be "seen" actually is. The microbes have cells, the cells have organelles and DNA, the organelles and DNA have compounds, the compounds have molecules, the molecules have atoms, the atoms have electrons, neutrons and photons, these components are materialized into the physical world due to the different types of photons. Even the photons dance in and out of the five-dimensional reality and are a result of other types of energetic patterns. They understood this back in India's 'ancient' Ayurvedic days. Now, even the term 'ancient' is taking on a different understanding as archeologists are discovering there were a huge number of civilizations, they had no awareness of, that make Atlantis seem like recent history. But I am getting sidetracked here. Let's get back on track.

In your era," and Merlin pointed to Jordan and Jasmine, "people are now becoming more aware and comfortable with an understanding of different types of energy. Most are coming back to an awareness that everything ultimately is made up of energy, but our brains are not organized to see the pure energy, only to pick up some of the frequencies and translate them into something 'meaningful'. People are starting to realize that like everything else, some energy is beneficial, and some is detrimental. A basic law of science is energy can never be created or destroyed, only changed. Yet despite the law, they still have virtually no idea about the true nature of energy. Kind of like when the 'scientists' believed in the absolute laws of gravity then found out gravity curves and didn't always abide by the laws they created.

Some scientists believe that once they understand all the different forms of energy; in the context of what is now called quantum energy and quantum physics, they will understand both the universe and the human condition. If on the other hand, they were real scientists, they would learn from their past false assumptions. Let's look at a few to give you an idea of how mankind keeps making the same mistakes over and over:

- Europeans believed the world was flat
- Ancient Greece and ancient China believed in 'geocentricity' meaning the earth was the center of the universe and everything in the universe revolved around it
- Looking to medicine, it was believed the body had four humors or fluids: blood, yellow bile, black bile and phlegm. When in balance a person was healthy; when out of balance a person became more and more sick. This concept was eliminated in the mid-1800s with the introduction of cellular biology

Or we could look at a few misconceptions just from your last 100 years, Jasmine and Jordan:

- 'Rain follows the plow', a belief that an increase in human settlement caused an increase in rainfall, or,
- Ice was the basic substance of everything, put forward by the Austrian Horbiger
- Water has 63 known anomalies and yet everyone thinks they understand the basic water compound. Actually, I correct myself; many are now going back to university to study water and attempt to figure out why the anomalies are there. They are starting to figure out why homeopathies can be so powerful.

The challenge I want you to embrace is every civilization has thought they were the most advanced; that they understood science, or magic, or whatever. It was as wrong in ancient Ayurveda times, as it was in Europe in the 12th century, as it is in the US in the 21st century. Medicine is as warped with as many falsehoods today as it ever was.

Pharmaceuticals kill as many people today as they always did, well actually even more. That Francis Crick guy who discovered DNA said..." Merlin paused attempting to get the quote correct, "...*and so to those of you who may be vitalists, I would make this prophecy: what everyone believed yesterday, and you believe today, only cranks will believe tomorrow.*" What he didn't seem to grasp was this can be said of all beliefs, throughout time," he looked directly at Jasmine, and this is particularly true of Western conventional medicine.

So, My Dear, you are very right to question it like you do. Keep questioning it as it is full of misconceptions. Germ theory itself, on which most of western medicine is based, is false. It is a theory that has come and gone throughout the ages and around the world, many times, to explain illness. Yet, it is so obvious. A 'germ' can only thrive in an environment that will support it. If the body produces a healthy environment for the human, only microbes supporting humans will be predominant and thrive there; if the body is producing an unhealthy environment, then microbes that are unhealthy to the body will thrive there. It is so basic yet so many just don't get it. But that is only one piece of a very complex puzzle.

Anyway, again I get off topic. When scientists gain a better comprehension of how the different types of energy function, it will simply open new doors to further levels of even more subtle frequencies that, as of yet, they have no comprehension of. They already have a relatively simple understanding that when you go past the big five: height, depth, width, time and space, there is no time and space. Good! Now their understanding still needs altering and modifying before they 'really' get it. Mankind has gone through these cycles of learning and understanding and appreciating many times before and they will cycle through it many times again. On the other hand, there have been those privileged ones, through the cycles of history, who have gone beyond and have learned. Those ones learned how to go beyond time and space and the very limited human senses, into other planes of 'reality'.

There are many problems with 'scientific evidence' or 'evidenced based science' in almost any field of study, medicine or otherwise. One of the problems is the 'street light effect'. Remember the drunken old man who lost his wallet and was looking for it underneath the street light? When asked where he thought he lost his wallet, he explained he thought he lost it on the other side of the street? When questioned as to why he was then looking for it over here under the street lamp, he answered, 'because it is easier to see in the light'. Another is 'follow the money'. People produce results to gain them more access to research funds, which of course provides them with an income. And yet another is basic false assumptions. Like using water as a reference when it has 63 anomalies they don't understand – talk about 'nuts'. The list goes on and on. This is why it is important that you go beyond the boundaries and limitations set up by false beliefs and assumptions which distort how studies are designed and analyzed.

Apart from medical sciences and astrophysics, one of my big issues is with psychological data. Take the mind. There is no agreement on what the mind is; therefore, there is no accepted definition, therefore no accepted measurement, yet we all accept it is there. They can't even agree as to whether the mind is an aspect of the brain; a result of the brain; an aspect of the energetic field; or if it impacts on the brain. There is so much they need to learn, it's almost funny. Take love. There is no agreement on what love is; there is no accepted definition; and there is no measurement for it; yet we all accept that we experience it. The list goes on and on. People may assume they live in a scientific era, but forget to question the basic tenets science holds, and unfortunately, most are wrong or incomplete or inadequate.

Oh dear, I have run off at the mouth once again. I do have a passion for going beyond; for questioning the accepted;

for expounding my favorite topics without ever shutting up. We need to get back on topic here.

The point is, remember to question; to push current beliefs; to move past your physical limitations and senses. There is so much more to life as you are already learning on some level. You have all learned to move past time and place and work with this level of awareness; this is only the beginning of your learning. There is so much more; how to manifest and create with thought and frequency, and how to access other levels of your being that exist on much higher, or subtler levels of frequencies. Listen, question, push to understand more than you think you know. No matter how far you go, there is always much further. Never be satisfied or content with what you think you know. On the other hand, learn acceptance. Accept there will always be more to learn. Don't get too caught up in the self, remember humor is truly a great medicine and a great way to keep objectivity.

Buddhist beliefs claim to truly love another or the self, you have to fully accept who the other/or self is, in the present; but always be pushing the other/or self to reach your greatest potential.

- Gandhi is known for saying "Be the change you want to see"
- Dr. Emoto for recognizing the connection between love and compassion
- Dr. Lipton for recognizing the connection between thought and DNA structure

They, and many others, have pieces you want to embrace. Just like each of you are pieces of the whole you. You also

164

need to connect with the Gibson's Clinic. They have a number of excellent practitioners that will really be able to help you a lot in your understanding. They will also be able to answer a lot of your medical based questions. Remember, your thoughts and actions can have impact on one another, both forward and backward across time. You have learned what it really means to draw from the past and gather from the future, though only on this plane, on the earth. You will eventually learn to go far beyond this plane. But we must be patient. Now we need to slip back into time and space, and when you wake up you will remember all of this. Work with it and remember to keep it in balance with the rest of your lives.

He drew them all together into a kind of hug. They were all energetic forms with given patterns, and yet, they were all one at the same time. It was a different and powerful experience, far removed from the physical hug of the earthly plane.

Chapter 31

Now What?

Jordan opened his eyes, "Holy shit!" he got up and moved around in the bed. Yes, he was in his body. No, he was not dreaming. He looked over to see if Jasmine was beside him. She was obviously awake as well. She kept opening her mouth to say something and then closing it again. He reached over and took her hand and squeezed it. It was unusual for Jasmine not to want to talk her way through understanding something but she wasn't saying anything.

'*Good,*' he thought to himself, he didn't want to talk either. He needed to think. He needed to go over what Merlin had said. Was it a dream? Was he being taught something? As much as Jasmine was there in his experience, did she perceive it the same way he did?

He got back into bed and laid down. They both just laid there for some time, just letting thoughts flow through their heads. Eventually Jordan rolled over to connect with Jasmine, but she put one hand up to stop him and squeezed his other hand. Jasmine didn't know what to do with the dream experience either, or whatever it was. It was too powerful for words. She needed to just lay there and be with it. To somehow allow her mind to absorb the experience, the information, Merlin, and do something with it she was not able to do on a conscious level. Finally, she rolled over to look at Jordan. "And you?" was all she said.

He simply shook his head, "I have no idea."

They laid there for the longest while, not saying anything else, just looking into each other's eyes, searching for answers to questions they did not know how to formulate. It seemed apparent they had a similar experience. Eventually, Jordan put an arm around Jasmine and pulled her close. He needed to feel her physical body against his. Still no words were formed, and they held the position for the longest time.

It was after lunch before they finally got out of bed and started to talk. Jasmine suggested they get their laptops and write down everything they could remember. Jordan agreed and suggested they not share anything until they had written everything down so as not influence one another. Jasmine simply nodded yes.

They got into their comfies and sat down at their desks. They typed and typed and typed. Though neither said a word, there was a lot of non-verbal sounds between them. Finally, Jasmine sat back with a sigh, "Do you want a coffee? I am not sure I could eat anything, but I think I need a coffee."

"Sounds great," Jordan responded absently; he was still typing. He continued for another 10 minutes while she made and brought him his coffee. When he was finished, he closed his laptop and turned to her, "I do love you, you know that, right?" For some reason this seemed an important thing to confirm, although he wasn't sure why.

"Yes, I do know that. And you know I love you too. But having said that, after last night, I am not really sure what that means."

"I know what you mean," he agreed, "although on the other hand, I am not sure what anything means anymore."

"Okay, so it sounds like we were in the same place last night, with Merlin?" she waited for his agreement, "Should we exchange notes to see how we each experienced it, remembered it, or dealt with it, or something? I am really baffled on how we should proceed with all of this."

"Um hmm," was all she got from him.

She raised her eyebrows, she needed something more. But if he was as perplexed as she was, she could understand how and why he didn't know how to continue either.

Then she started to laugh, he looked up at her with a raised eyebrow in question, "What's so funny?"

"Well I just wondered what the other ones, or the other parts of us, or whatever, are doing. Are they as confused with all of this as we are? Have they had discussions about this we aren't aware of? Are they more familiar with all Merlin teaches than we are? Hey, if we are all really one, or at least if all three women are one, maybe we are all one? Whatever, it would be cool if we could just do a Dr. Spock 'mind meld' kind of thing. That would be great for learning, as well as, for sharing experiences."

"Yeah, yeah, that would be cool, but back up. You have a point there. Really, if we are all just an energetic frequency, is it that we are actually one woman and one man between the six of us? Or is it that we are all six of us, actually one? Or if we went further than that, are we all six of us one with Merlin? Where do the boundaries lie? Can we define our boundaries and meld them when we want? Oh man, I don't know if my head can handle all of this. Do you want to go for a walk or something?"

"Yeah maybe that's a good idea. But I really do wish I knew what the others were doing with all of this. It might help me figure out what I am to do with it all."

They got changed and went for a walk. Intermittently they asked questions, perhaps more of the self than of the other. Then they were silent again for long periods.

It was important for Jordan to hold Jasmine's hand, somehow he felt it kept him grounded, although he really wasn't' sure why. When he would get really baffled in his thoughts, he would come blurt out, "You know I love you, don't you?"

Didn't Merlin say the more solid something was, the more of an illusion it was? Were they illusions of reality; was their love; what was real? The thought just kept getting more esoteric and confusing.

"Oh, I have an idea," Jasmine burst out, all of a sudden, "what if we meditate to connect with the others to find out what they are doing with all this?" It continued to seem so important to know what the others were doing with it. Was she just being nosey? Was it to get direction? Was it the need to have someone else she could talk with, because there sure wasn't anyone here she could go to? She wasn't sure why she needed that connection, but it just kept coming up for her.

"Okay, when we get back we can try. But man, even that seems too much. I am really having a very difficult time with all of this. I don't want them to add even more stuff I can't handle." He wasn't complaining, just acknowledging the over whelm.

"If we really are all one, then we should be able to help one another, shouldn't we?"

"I get your point, on the other hand, what if they are just as challenged with it all, as we are?"

"On the other hand, they all seemed to have more awareness of this stuff than we do. They have worked with it longer. We are the greenhorns." Jasmine was sure they could help.

"They have been around a lot longer than we have."

"Why are there never any finished answers, just more questions?"

"Now you are getting it. Remember, acceptance." a voice said.

Both of them looked around to see who said that. "You heard that too?" Jordan wanted to make sure he wasn't going mad.

"Yeah," she laughed, "that was Merlin."

"You do know schizophrenics hear voices too?"

"Yes, but in this case we both heard the voice, and we both recognized the voice, and the voice gave good direction. Let's go find the others."

Chapter 32

Love and Laughter

They went back to the condo and into position in their normal meditation corner with pillows and blankets. In moments, they were both in another realm.

"We have been waiting for you. You guys are sure slow," Jasmini laughed at them.

"And you were waiting for us, because...?" Jasmine wanted to know.

"You guys have been asking a lot of questions within yourselves and between yourselves. What we all went through last night was not entirely unknown to the four of us, but we knew it would be heavy duty for you. And you are right, we are all here to work together on this. We are all part of the same energetic, pattern," Jasmini nodded to Jordan, "which is why you hear statements from the sages of the past saying, "we are all one". We are all one on a given level, however on other levels, we have unique patterns, like you were thinking.

Similarly, with the six of us, we are all one, though each of us has a unique energetic pattern. We are able to blend those energies or keep them separate, depending on what we want to do with them. Take for instance, baking breads, initially the eggs and flours and milk and baking powder are separate, then they can be blended into one. The difference on the physical plane is once you blend those ingredients, or energies, you cannot take them back to their original form; whereas we have the capacity to move back and forth.

So yes, the three women who are here, although there are many, many forms of us, are separate and as one. Likewise, with our male counterparts, and just as Jordan asked; the six of us together, males and females, are also one. Then with Merlin, on another plane, we are all one with Merlin. Simply put, the higher up you go, or the subtler the energy you deal with, the more you can blend and/or remain separate, as you wish.

To answer another of your questions, there are many forms of more and more subtle energies. In other realms, we have different terms for it, but "energies" works for now. Eventually you get to a place where life is simple awareness, without energy. On earth, they still have an old Newtonian carbon-based life definition. As you grow and learn, you realize there are many different forms of life not carbon based; then there are even more forms of life that have nothing to do with chemicals. Many of our great Masters know how to move back and forth across these different levels and have taught us much, but your 'Western' societies have blocked out this understanding in the name of 'science'. What Western scientists don't realize is 'science' has evolved much further than where it currently is in your time; evolved many times; and has also gone backwards, many times. Unfortunately, a lot of what you call 'science' today is once again moving backwards, as it usually does when it gets driven by greed and power rather than by a need for truth and understanding. But that's a discussion for another time.

The point of coming back here now, is so you know you can draw on us at any time. We are all here for one another. Reach out, do not isolate yourself. The universe, or at least this universe, has bountiful and unlimited resources. Suffering in silence can lead to insanity. The mind gets boggled in on itself and loses its way out; whereas when we reach out in love and compassion, the universe offers us not only understanding but love and compassion in return."

The others were all sitting quietly with smiles of compassion and understanding, while Jasmini talked and explained. "We can only be of help to you if you reach out to us. And because you are a part of us, we want to help as much as we can. Remember, we know when it is novel and new, it can be overwhelming and confusing. Believe me, we know, we have all been there. Over time it becomes second nature and just part of the process; we have all been there as well. You might also want to remember it is your, or our, capacity for 'love and laughter' bringing us all to this level of development. Keep this in the forefront when struggling to come to terms with it all; love and laughter."

Chapter 33

Intent and Purpose

Jasmine opened her eyes and rolled over onto her side, laughing, "I love it. They answered so many of our questions from this morning, and we didn't even have to ask. In a sense we manifested that experience. Now I am going to go through my whole life, from this point on, manifesting my life with purpose and intent and filling it with love, compassion and laughter." She rolled over onto her back and stretched like a cat. Rather than her eyes being full of dark confusion, concern and question; she was now full of light, enthusiasm and laughter. She looked up at Jordan and stretched her arms out to him, inviting him to join her in a hug and a new perspective.

"You are right, My Lady. Hey, our My Lord and My Lady terms probably come from Jordian and Juliana. And I bet she is a 'Wanton Witch' too," he rolled down onto the floor beside her and took her in his arms. There was a hugely different energy between them now. "Oh, life is going to be a very interesting journey this time around. I am so thankful we found one another."

"Hey, I wonder if we have ever been with anyone else in other lifetimes. Now wouldn't that be interesting? Would you get jealous, My Lord, or would I be jealous?" she asked more of herself. "I think having gone through what we have to this point, I could never be jealous. What would be the point? It would just be another aspect of our journey. An interesting thought."

"I think we need to go and have a shower, wash off all the questions and concerns; lather each other in soap suds and love; then move in a very different direction than we did this morning. Are you up for it?"

Jasmine was already up and running ahead of him, "Beat you there," she challenged as she pulled off her clothes, leaving them in the hallway behind her.

He was doing the same as he struggled to get ahead of her. As they moved into the ensuite, he wrapped his arms around her as if to hug her to him, but as she reached up for his kiss, he stepped into the shower ahead of her. Raising his arms above his head he exclaimed in triumphant victory, "I won."

All the tense energy of the morning was being recycled into laughter and fun as they played and teased each other and washed away all their concerns. They had long ago decided this shower was really too small to make love in. So, Jasmine positioned herself and made ready for the mad dash to the bed. She was determined to get there first. She pushed him back into the shower with her behind and made the dash for the bed, "I won, I won," she exclaimed as she kneeled on the bed and stretched one arm up in victory.

"Oh, and do I love it when you celebrate your victory in naked splendor, with a lovely breast reaching out and begging for my attention," Jordan slid onto the bed alongside her, pushing her wet body back onto the sheets.

He held her one arm up while he took the lovely taunt nipple into his mouth. They played and wrestled and tickled and laughed their way through making love. It was such a good place to be.

Satiated, they rolled into one another. Jasmine wrapped an arm around him and held his butt. Jordan draped his arm around her and pulled her close, "God, I don't think I could get through all of this without you. And now we have the rest of our lives to work with this stuff and help make the world a better place." he committed to her.

Chapter 34

Jasmine, Juliana and Jasmini

Jasmini, Jasmine and Juliana were all very careful not to get caught up in their night time activities. They had to teach and guide children, live lives, tend gardens, help heal clients, work in their hospitals or clinics and do a huge number of day to day things.

Eventually, Jasmine and Jordan grew accustomed to their double life. There was so much Merlin could teach them. Every time he pulled back a layer of the onion, he revealed even more forcing their minds to broaden so they could embrace the lessons. They moved back and forth across time, to other life times. They watched and learned what they had already learned in previous lives or what they were to learn in future lives. The biggest impact was how it allowed their souls to develop lessons about love; about forgiveness; about compassion; about acceptance; and about what happened when you eliminated polarized thinking. All the lessons opened them up for even deeper lessons to further expand their understanding including how to move through different subtle energies and back again and the differences in perceptions as one moved; lessons about how to use energy in a positive constructive way, ways going past 'positive thinking' which was the current big hit in Jordan and Jasmine's time.

On the material plane, Juliana learned a lot about the 'healing magic' of the herbs she worked with and she learned about the Eastern herbs Jasmini worked with.

Jasmini knew a lot more about all the different processes used in combining and formulating herbs. More importantly, Merlin had taught her to work with them energetically which was very different from how herbalists worked in Juliana's era. On the other hand, she learned, about the different compounds in the herbs she was already using from Jasmine's era. It was funny to watch healers in Jasmine's era. They would isolate one compound from these beautiful plants and try to recreate them in a laboratory then actually expect they would have a similar effect.

As much as Jasmine had studied Conventional medicine of the 20th century, she was learning a tremendous amount about foods and herbs and what they could do to eliminate disease. And of course, she had the ability to research the website for new information they were learning about the different compounds in the plants. Eventually, she to working with aspects from her future and learned how future generations thought Western conventional medicine from Jasmine's time was outright barbaric. They recognized older healing modalities were much further ahead than 20th century medicine in so many ways.

Once Jasmine's started working with Juliana, the two became very close. They had different personalities in the different lifetimes. This was a funny thing to think as they were actually the same person. When she worked with Jasmini, she had a different kind of closeness. How could you have a different kind of closeness with different aspects of the self? Yet, she thought as she became more aware of herself, in all of her dimensions, wasn't she closer to given aspects of the self in a given dimension? Sometimes the questions themselves got awfully complicated.

Jasmini started working with Juliana before Jasmine joined the group and added a huge amount of information from her Ayurveda training. She had a somewhat different personality again.

From one perspective they were all the same; from another they were all unique. Jasmine was the courageous one who wanted to save the world by going out and working on international projects with her future husband, Jordan.

Juliana was quite content to have the world come to her. She loved her barraca, her gardens, and her children. She made her tinctures and balms and other remedies; and the world came to her.

Jasmini was the gentlest of the three. She didn't want to go into the world; she didn't want the world to come her; she left all the sick people to her father and her husband. She was happiest attending her garden and making the remedies for others to use.

Jasmini and her husband were still working on creating children; Juliana and her husband already had her three; and Jasmine and her husband didn't want any. Their focus was to volunteer for projects around the world and they often discussed whether it would be a benefit, or detriment, to raise children that way, besides the world was over populated. If they did decide to have children, they thought it would be much more logical, and romantic, to adopt a child who desperately needed a home. There were millions of orphaned and abandoned children around the world who needed homes. It just made so much more sense to be part of the solution and bring one of those children into their home, rather than add to the problem, by contributing to over population.

Chapter 35

Projects Around the World

As the years went by, Jasmine and Jordan did work on many projects. Eventually they tried to organize their life to go away for two months a year on a project.

Jasmine continued to work for the same hospital. The project works she did was a big marketing component for her hospital and they gave her the time, plus she always brought back the pictures they wanted.

As Jordan's company developed, he received more and more contracts for 'Green' hospitals, homes, and even orphanages. He worked with institutions around the world and developed a huge name for himself. His work lent itself well to the projects they chose to work on. He would help clients design and build the buildings; while Jasmine helped to bring medicine to the families.

Jasmine became well recognized for her abilities to know and understand the foods, herbs and spices of a given culture and how to use them to help heal the people. Merlin had taught her that people should eat the foods grown in their own region. A person's metabolism and healing ability was connected to the foods and herbs grown in that region. In addition, it allowed the people to get engaged in their own culture, while they were healing.

A future aspect of Jasmine shared how 20th century medicine was perceived. It wasn't much different than when the Catholic Church went in and wiped out a culture replacing the belief systems and culture with that of the church; or when the Muslims did a similar process, of again wiping out other people's cultures believing everyone should operate the way they did. When one country, religion or medicine has the power to strip another culture of their way of doing things, they can bring both good and bad. In the future, the Western Conventional medicine of the 20th century was considered vulgar and crude, synthetic and artificial, and incredibly arrogant. Although like other invaders, along the way, it did bring some good.

Jasmine understood what her future aspect shared with her. She shared much of the same beliefs in her own era. It pushed her to help the people of each project learn about their own agriculture, vegetation, food and herbs. What was healing and beneficial; what was toxic and destructive. And, of course, she had the help of her other aspects to learn, what she needed to know.

Their life was full and abundant. Whether they called him Merlin or Babaji, he stayed with all of them and continued to guide and teach them. One of the things they all learned repeatedly, was the more you gave, the more you received, but only when the attitude of giving and helping others was behind the giving. If the attitude behind the giving was to get, it developed a negative impact.

They also learned tone and attitude have a huge impact on words exchanged; intent and purpose have a huge impact on behavior; and beliefs can either restrict or expand your capacity to grow and learn. Underneath it all, is the capacity for love. To love the self and to love the other who is ultimately part of the self is huge. The deeper the love, the greater the ability for that love to cross time.

And as Jasmine and Jordan lay on the beach, underneath the warm afternoon sun, they knew they had a love that crosses time. .

Afterword

Normally an epilogue is provided to take the reader into the future and create closure of topics from within the novel.

This is not a normal epilogue. I am writing it to provide information from the future about the author, me. I wrote this book while on a holiday in the Dominican Republic. It was a very strange experience. The book was not at all what I had intended to write, when I began the book. I normally write books in a very sequential fashion. This book, however, was written in a very erratic fashion, and I had no idea where the thoughts and ideas were coming from or how it was going to come together. Not only had I not intended three couples, or Merlin, but there were ideas and concepts that I had never thought of that were included in the book.

While writing the book, I kept laughing. "It "felt" like someone else was writing the book. Just plain weird. When I got home and explained the experience to friends and family, everyone said, "The book was channeled". An interesting concept and certainly one I was familiar with concept, but me? Why? It became a topic we just laughed about.

I finally got around to doing the editing three years later. A lot had happened in my life during that time. Most predominantly, my partner crossed over and took me on the most bizarre journey of my life.

During that year, I was working overboard. Needing to grieve the loss of my mother, then three weeks later my partner; then three weeks later the house sold, then I had to start building the new house already planned and contracted. I had to pack and unpack both my household, twice as I had to live with a friend temporarily while the new house was being built, and my father's home and my offices.

In addition, I was a director on several boards and very active in several different networking programs. I wrote three books with my partner and four other books. And of course, I had to continue seeing clients; doing research; preparing protocols.

I already had several books that needed publication. Several books from the Entwined Collection were on hold, as I had just started to look for someone to create the covers when my partner crossed over.

And now I was writing a whole other series of books regarding my partner and what he was sharing with me from his journey on the other side. It was a bizarre journey that I needed to come to terms with both cognitively and emotionally. After my partner crossed over, he taught me to communicate with him, on the other side. That was an awesome journey in and of itself!!! And that journey provided the basis for Tom's Collection.

The journey, the books about the journey, the covers for the books all had to be dealt with amidst a huge amount of work I was doing in this plane of existence, we like to think of as reality.

Finally, I got back on track. I hired Christine to edit the books; Peter to create the covers of the books; and Leah to start working on the formatting and publishing. Books were getting edited and covers were being created and it was time to edit Christine's editing of this book from three years before. Wow! What a surprise.

Over the intermediate years, thoughts would randomly come to be about how I should organize the book differently. Or, parts that I should expand on and other parts that needed to be shorter. When I started to edit the book, it was not organized as I thought I had organized it. Parts that I thought I would have to develop were already developed. And parts I thought I would have to shorten were already done. The male partner, throughout the book, was my partner! His characteristics and the dynamics were us. What happened when they moved into different realms, were similar to what my partner was now telling me!

As I continued to read through the book, I stopped editing it and just simply read it. I had goose bumps going up and down my arms and my back. It was "freaky"! There was so much, I had no recall of that was so indicative of my partner and my myself. We were not even romantically involved when I wrote the book! Yet, umpteen dynamics and issues and characteristics in the book, were us!

It repeatedly brought tears to my eyes as I continued to read through the book. I kept sharing with my friends, "Look at what I wrote! It's amazing?"

In the first book, Tom: The Cosmic Socialite, Merlin came through and claimed that he had "channeled" this book! Wow! Really! The fact that I was communicating with Tom was bizarre enough, but Merlin?? Anyways, whether you chose to believe it or not, in my experience, Merlin claimed that he had channeled the book and there were parts I was missing and that we would work together again!

At the point of editing this book, this has not happened yet. However, when I questioned Tom about what was going on, the following conversation occurred:

Me: Hi there, I am working on Maria's book, A Love that Crosses Time. It is awesome; I don't recall half of what is in there. So much of it alludes to you, and to you and me – it is like it is a premonition. Holy shit!

Tom: Yes. You are right. Merlin is here.

Me: Hi…I am in awe. Wow. I knew that was a weird experience writing the book.

Merlin: Well my dear, I told you I channeled it for you. I knew when you started to edit it you would be amazed. There is a lot there, I channeled it to prepare you for Tom and this work. You have done well.

Me: I don't know what to say, this is so bizarre. I know you told me you channeled the book and I certainly know it was a strange book to write.

Merlin: Well we have a lot of work to do. Hang in there.

Tom: He's gone. That was quick. But I am working on the book with you - it is interesting. You are obviously gifted.

Again, whether you chose to believe this or not is obviously up to you. I can only share what my experience was. For me it was bizarre and yet so full of love.

Members of the Entwined Book Project

Smiths: Married for 23 years at the age of 24 and 25, October 25

Name: Maria, 47
Book: A Love that Crosses Time
Issue: Adrenal Fatigue
Character: Realtor that is a go getter, but family is most important; loves husband dearly

Name: Duncan, 48
Book: A Book for Men: How to Create a Good Marriage
Issue: Enlarged left ventricle
Character: Devoted husband and father

Name: Jessie, 20, daughter
Book: Female Sexuality
Issue: Diabetes
Character: University student, initially wants to be an MD but moves into Real Medicine, boyfriend Steve

Name: Jasmine, 15, daughter
Book: A Time Travel Romance
Issue: Asthma
Character: Dancer, somewhat shy, boyfriend Nick

Name: John, 9, son
Book: How Aliens Would Interpret our Planet
Issue: Allergies
Character: Artist, loves Granddad

Friends

Name: Steve, 20, Jessie's boyfriend
Book: How to Deal with Alcoholic Husbands
Issue: Alcoholic father
Character: University student, father alcoholic, submissive mother, avoids home-life, loves the Smith family

Name: Nick, 15, Jasmine's boyfriend
Book: Music, Sound & Other Energies for Healing
Character: Dancer, somewhat shy, Steve is like an older brother

Maria's Parents
Name: Grandma Mary
Book: Manage or Eliminate Arthritis
Issue: Arthritis
Character: Sweet; grandma type; adores grandpa

Name: Papa Johnny
Book: The Politics of Health
Issue: Dementia
Character: Funny old guy; set in his ways, but changing his mind

Maria's sister Carol and family
Name: Carol, Maria's sister
Book: Emotional Eating
Issue: Weight
Character: Kind of belligerent; but wants the best for her family
Husband George

Name: George, Maria's brother-in-law
Book: Covering Up Suicidal Thinking
Issue: Depression
Character: He's tries to be the man; but really isn't; not confident like Duncan; but holds his own with his wife Carol

Name: Tim, 19, Maria's nephew
Book: What it Feels Like NOT to be Understood
Issue: Paranoia
Character: Weak; not well developed; insecure, girlfriend Shelley

Name: Sherry, 15, Maria's niece
Book: A Romance About Gaining Self Control
Issue: Obsessive-Compulsive
Character: Struggles with control issues, boyfriend Randy

Name: Shelley
Book: Teen Age Empowerment
Issue:
Character: Tim's girlfriend

Maria's brother Dave and family

Name: Dave, Maria's brother
Book: When Enough is Enough
Issue: Divorce
Character: Dave compassionate man; gives too much; finally divorced bipolar abusive Joan

Grandma Mary's brother and family

Name: Dan
Book: How to Design Your Dream Home
Issue: High cholesterol, hyper -tension
Character: He's a good guy; but private; hasn't dated anyone
since his wife Judy died years ago

Gibson family – own the Gibsons Clinic

Name: Dr Jim
Book: Personality Styles & Marriage
Character: Psychotherapist Social/outgoing; fun but wise,
Julie's husband

Name: Julie
Book: A Book comparing East & West Religious
Philosophies
Character: Physiotherapist, gentle; sweetheart; nurturing,
Jim's wife

Name: Dr Jane
Book: A New Integrative Model for Cellular Healing
Character: Dr of Natural Medicine Academic; knows her
stuff; confident in her knowledge
Gibson's daughter

Name: Dr Daniel
Book: A Very Unique Cookbook
Character: PhD Nutrition, academic but has fun with food,
Gibson's son

Name: Nanny Sarah
Book: Romance and Cerebral Palsy
Character: Acupuncturist, gentle, nurturing, mothering,
accommodating, Jim's mother

Name: Pappy
Book: Eliminating Autism
Character: Master Herbalist, fun, happy go lucky, loves life,
Jim's father

.

Dr. Holly Additional Resources

Dr. Holly is an International Speaker on weekly and monthly radio and TV programs. She presents at Conferences and Workshops Internationally.

Listen to her on one of her regular talk shows: www.NewsForTheSoul.com and on various other talk shows you can access through her site, www.ChoicesUnlimited.ca

Read her writings on several Internet programs as well as her own website: www.ChoicesUnlimited.ca

When she is not presenting, writing, or consulting, Dr. Holly spends her time researching health.

Her books, videos, and free downloads can be found on www. Dr.HollyBooks.com

51462905R00117

Made in the USA
Columbia, SC
19 February 2019